# RUTHLESS
## as HELL

Once, a long time ago,

a beautiful angel

fell in love with

a sinful demon...

# RUTHLESS AS HELL
## THE DEMON ACADEMY
### BOOK TWO

G. BAILEY

# CONTENTS

| | |
|---|---|
| Description | xiii |
| Prologue | 1 |
| Chapter 1 | 5 |
| *Knocking on the door of hell* | |
| Chapter 2 | 13 |
| *Is there a return label for Lucifer?* | |
| Chapter 3 | 24 |
| *The demon has come out to play* | |
| Chapter 4 | 32 |
| *The heart is an easy thing to break* | |
| Chapter 5 | 39 |
| *Someone needs coffee in the morning* | |
| Chapter 6 | 51 |
| *Jealousy is a cruel mistress* | |
| Chapter 7 | 55 |
| *Death by a flying horse* | |
| Chapter 8 | 64 |
| *The angels have a pretty castle; how is that fair?* | |
| Chapter 9 | 79 |
| *A long drive with Satan. Heaven save me please* | |
| Chapter 10 | 88 |
| *I'm sure the fairy tale said to run from the wolf, not kiss him* | |
| Chapter 11 | 97 |
| *Knock once for hell, two for...* | |
| Chapter 12 | 106 |
| *A demon and a wolf are drinking in a pub...* | |

### Chapter 13
*Never make a deal with the devil. You will regret it* — 119

### Chapter 14
*Kiss me like nothing else in the world matters* — 127

### Chapter 15
*One more puzzle to add to the box* — 137

### Chapter 16
*Who would win in a fight? Wolf or Demon?* — 144

### Chapter 17
*The price of lies* — 150

### Chapter 18
*Welcome home...or maybe not* — 156

### Chapter 19
*Born in fire? Ouch...* — 165

### Chapter 20
*The day I've been waiting for* — 175

### Chapter 21
*Death be a trial tonight...* — 185

### Chapter 22
*Five in the bed, and the little one said...* — 194

### Chapter 23
*A letter from the dead* — 200

### Chapter 24
*Why don't stubborn boys say sorry?* — 205

### Chapter 25
*May the true alpha rule.* — 210

### Chapter 26
*The time the angel met the wolf* — 217

### Chapter 27
*The demon cat.* — 224

### Chapter 28
*Death is just the beginning...* — 228

### Epilogue — 232

### Note From The Author. — 235

| | |
|---|---|
| About the Author | 237 |
| Other Books by G. Bailey | 239 |
| Excerpt from Wings of Ice. | 241 |
| Bonus Read of Wings of Ice | 245 |
| 29. Bonus read | 249 |
| 30. Bonus read | 276 |
| 31. Bonus read | 284 |

Ruthless as Hell © 2019 G. Bailey

This is a work of fiction. Names, characters, places, and incidents either are the products of the author's imagination or are used fictitiously.
Any resemblance to actual persons, living or dead, businesses, companies, events, or locales is entirely coincidental.
All Rights Reserved. No part of this book may be reproduced or used in any manner without the express written permission of the publisher except for the use of brief quotations in a book review.

Edits by Polished Perfection

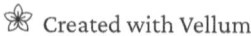 Created with Vellum

# DESCRIPTION

**I can't escape this academy...**
My name is Lexi Cameron, and I really need some help in the form of two sexy demons, an alpha's wayward son, and an angel who is worse than the fallen.
*The only (tiny) problem?*
They'd rather kill me than help me get out of here.
Welcome to Demon Academy, where the students might do more than just try to kill you. They might give your soul to hell and smile as they wave goodbye.
Funny enough, I think mine belongs there anyway.

*That is if Lucifer has anything to do with it...*
RH Dark Academy Romance. 18+

# PROLOGUE

## LILITH (ROYAL CONSORT OF THE KING OF HELL)

18 YEARS AGO...

"Please. Please don't take them!" I scream at the beautiful monster standing over me, holding my sweet little boys in his arms. I should have known not to trust him. I should have run away when they were still in my belly, when they were safe. Their dark curly hair is all I can see as he hides them in the woven white blankets I made for them. *My boys. My sweet princes.* Thick tears fall off my cheeks as I pull against the chains on my wrists and ankles, feeling more frantic and desperate than ever before in my long life. "Please. I'm their mother!"

"And I am their father. It is my choice, and they are not welcome in hell any longer," he replies, his voice void of any emotion. I stare into his eyes, remembering the angel who fell into hell for me all those thousands of years ago.

The angel I would have happily died for.

The angel who is now stealing my baby boys.

"They will not challenge you. Please, Lucifer. Please." My pleas are nothing to him, and we both know it. Many people have pleaded for their lives or their loved ones' lives, at his feet, and he has never once given them what they wanted.

I am no different.

My beautiful boys are no more than a few months old, and already I sense such power in them. Every moment they spend in hell, the stronger they become. If they were brought up here, then they could rival their father in power.

Lucifer will never allow that. He will never allow a fallen angel to live in hell, to challenge his power. My sweet boys are fallen, their births here made that choice.

Even a half fallen angel is a threat to Lucifer.

And Lucifer knows it. My boys cry as Lucifer stands ever so still, fire curling up around him as he starts to take them away. I will never see them again, and the pain of that thought nearly stops my heart altogether.

"Please let me say goodbye. Please." I need to tell them their mother loves them. That I will find a way to go to earth and be in their lives. *I will find a way.* I just need to tell—

"You are bound to hell, my precious demon consort. This is your price for luring me here all those years ago. Break it, and we both know the price you will pay." He disappears with my children as my heart breaks into a million pieces, and I scream so loudly even earth can hear me all the way from hell.

# CHAPTER ONE

KNOCKING ON THE DOOR OF HELL

"The King of Hell requests your presence." The Heller's words are spoken so calmly and almost normally, even though the actual words incite nothing other than fear from me. My mouth is dry as I eye the three Hellers standing behind the one who spoke outside my room, and it is very clear that they will make me go and see him if I refuse. My hand shakes as I nod, gripping the cold doorknob in my hand as I pull my front door closed, and the Hellers circle themselves around me, like they expect me to make a run for it.

If I were leaving, I would have flipping sure as hell gone a lot sooner. I wipe my tired eyes, pushing away the few tears gathered there as we walk through the empty academy. There is utter silence, which is a good change from the screams of wolves I've listened to all night as I ran around the academy, getting any wolves I could find to go to Claus and Nikoli's room.

They promised to get them out. I just have to believe they are true to their word, even though I'm not their mate like they thought.

Why does it hurt so much I'm not their mate?

I'm not sure I ever wanted it to begin with. I still shake from the events of last night; I still can't stop picturing it all like a bad movie. Over and over again. Never stopping, never giving me a break.

It's all real. I'm meant to be the Queen of Hell and rule at Lucifer's side.

Over my dead body is that happening any time soon. We walk past the statue, the one I stop and stare at. I know why it's familiar now. It was him all along, ever since I met him in that restaurant.

I had a date with the devil, and I didn't even know it.

"Move!" the Heller on my right shouts at me,

and I cross my arms, pressing them against the satin dress I'm still wearing. I somewhat hate it now as it only serves to remind me of that awful night. It is torn in places, and I have no doubt my hair looks in a similar state, as I've been running around the academy. The Heller goes to grab my arm, and I curl my fist as I dodge him, knowing if he touches me, I'm going to punch him.

"I will take Miss Cameron from here." Mr. Morganach's statement makes me feel like I can breathe for the first time in hours, his voice pulling me into a sense of safety. The Hellers all turn to look at Morgan as he walks to us, his white shirt crisp and perfect, his hair wavy and styled to the right, and his black trousers tightly fitted. Morgan doesn't look at me as he stares down the nervous Hellers, who don't bother arguing with him before they run off together, and I try to take in every bit of Morgan. Everything from his green eyes that look like uncut emeralds that people would pay thousands to just touch, to his strong jawline, to his beckoning lips. Mr. Morganach is what any woman could ever want in a man on the outside, but on the inside, he is all kinds of fucked up. He knows it, which makes it worse, and I know it, which makes me crazy for falling for him.

Morgan is addictive, that is all there is to it. He makes you want to find out more, makes you want to understand and fix his fucked-up heart. If that is even possible. I like to think I stand a chance. I'm falling for my teacher, *how messed up is that*?

Morgan inclines his head towards the lift, and we walk over, meeting side by side in front of the closed lift. I step closer to Mr. Morganach's side, almost naturally, as he presses the button for the lift. I try not to look directly at him as we wait for the lift, but it's a losing fight as I look, meeting his green eyes, finding him staring right at me.

He looks furious.

And I never want to look away. I should be scared; anyone in their right mind would be utterly terrified of Morgan right in this moment.

Not me and my stupid heart. *We like it.*

My heart beats fast as the lift doors open, and we go inside, silent as the doors softly close. The second they do, Morgan's hands cup my cheeks as he steps in front of me.

"Are you alright, baby?" he demands.

"Define alright?" I counter, and he smirks for a second until that second is over and the situation we are in comes crashing back. Both of us are silent because the truth is, nothing is alright anymore. One second we were dancing and Morgan was admitting real feelings for me, and the next, our world was blown up.

Now we have to admit that it's not just him and me anymore. We have the flipping devil in the way.

"Whatever this fucking asshole tells you, don't believe it. Don't trust him," he tells me, each word firmer than the last. "And you are not his. No way is that happening. I'd rather see you with his messed-up sons than Lucifer."

"I'm not going to trust the devil, Morgan," I softly tell him, knowing he needs to calm down before he blows up in this elevator. He steps away from me, his hands curled into fists and his wings fluttering almost angrily behind him. I slam my hand on the emergency stop button on the wall, making the lift stop and the lights flicker as Morgan looks at me. I step forward and gently place my hands on his shoulders. He doesn't move. He closes his eyes as I stroke my hands up over his shoulders and to his wings.

Running my hands over the ridges and feathers, I'm surprised that they are far softer than I thought they would be.

"Do you trust me?" Morgan asks me as I continue to touch his wings, knowing Morgan is asking something else at the same time. It's not just trust, it's love.

Not that he would ever ask me that directly. Not that he loves me anyway. I'm not sure he knows how to love someone after all these years of only loving himself.

"Not in the same way, I suspect," I tell him, and he opens his eyes, and for almost a full second, he looks on the edge of saying something more before he is serious again. The change of his features is hard to miss when you know him like I do. "We could leave right now. I will take you somewhere safe."

"I can't. My parents need me, and I will not leave them to their deaths without a witness," I tell him, moving my hands away and stepping back. Morgan all but glowers at me.

"You said you don't remember anything. You can't help them if Lucifer kills you," he warns me. I might not remember what they need me to, but I can tell the demon leaders how they are good people and how they would never kill five friends and take their souls.

"Lucifer doesn't want me dead. He wants something far worse," I remind Morgan.

"Then use that to stay alive while I make a plan to get us out of here. Play his game and fucking win it," he firmly tells me, his voice thick with overprotectiveness and an urge to get me the hell out of here. "And I will always be around the corner. You just call for me, and I will be there."

"Does anyone ever win a game against the devil, Morgan?" I enquire as Morgan slams the emergency button and the lift starts going up once again.

"The devil is just an angel who fell into hell. A fallen angel, nothing more," Morgan reminds me. "He may have broken the rules, he may have gone where no angel ever should have, but that does not make him a king. The only reason he is king is because no one has ever gone to hell and killed him."

"So he was like you once," I muse. "Does falling into hell make angels more powerful?"

"Once," Morgan answers as the lift stops. "We lose our wings for power the second we step into hell. I never understood why anyone would fly into hell knowing you would lose your wings. It would be like losing a part of yourself." The doors open the moment Morgan stops speaking, not giving me a chance to reply. I don't understand why Lucifer flew into hell all those years ago. I believe he did it for the twins' mum, a demon he was in love with.

Is love a reason to jump into hell? Even knowing the price?

We step out onto a floor I haven't been on before, where there is nothing more than smooth white tiles and a pair of large glossy red doors with three Hellers in front of it. These Hellers are a little different as they have red star pentagrams on their cloak arms in lines from the shoulder down to the wrist, and the swords catching the light under their cloaks look deadly. Morgan walks out of the elevator with me, each one of our footsteps on the tiles seeming like it echoes. It's frightening. We get to the doors, where we stop in front of them, and I look up at Morgan just once. Once is enough.

"The King of Hell will see you now."

Flipping great.

## CHAPTER
# TWO

IS THERE A RETURN LABEL FOR LUCIFER?

It takes the King of Hell a long time to open the damn door, considering he invited us here, and the Hellers seem to think he wants to see us now, but they won't let us walk in. In the time we wait in silence, I think about whether it would be worth it to go back to my room as he can't be bothered to answer the door.

Would it be worth running away and hoping he can never find me rather than making it easy for him?

Then the door suddenly opens, and I god damn wish it didn't. Lucifer stands holding the door open, literally naked as the day he was born, I suspect. I don't look down past his neck, focusing on his stupidly handsome face and wavy, damp blond hair. He looks like the twins; I see it so clearly now where I never did before.

The twins are more handsome, more real. Lucifer looks like the Ken doll my mum bought me so my Barbie could have a boyfriend. I never liked the Ken doll, and neither did Barbie. She liked having her Barbie mansion all to herself.

Same can be said of The Demon Academy and me. I don't want Lucifer here.

"Are clothes not a fashion in hell?" I sarcastically ask before I can make myself shut up. Lucifer laughs, a deep, throaty laugh that makes me tense up. I doubt that is the reaction he gets from any other girl.

"My mate is amusing. I was just in the shower. Do come in, Alexandria," he suggests, stepping back and holding the door open for me. I take a deep breath before stepping into the hallway, and I spin around to see Lucifer stand between Morgan and me.

"Mr. Morganach, the angel I've heard of who is working here as punishment?" Lucifer asks, eyeing Morgan, and Morgan stares right back. The room becomes so thick with tension that every single little noise seems amplified. Everything from the water dropping off Lucifer onto the tiles, to the heavy breathing of one of the Hellers. I can hear the rain outside, the stormy weather that never leaves us.

"Correct," Morgan angrily utters, making the room even more tense.

"Why are you escorting my mate?" Lucifer demands. Morgan moves his gaze to me, leisurely running his eyes over my body before back to Lucifer.

*I'm sure that made things less tense.*

"The Hellers are shit at protecting anything, let alone the soon to be Queen of Hell. I am much better," Morgan smoothly replies. "I am her teacher and personal trainer after all."

"Interesting," Lucifer comments, looking briefly at me, and I quickly hide my emotions, making them as neutral as I can get them when Morgan is around. "Mr. Morganach, come and see me in a few hours. As for now, you are not needed, and thank you for protecting my mate from the dangers of...a lift," he adds, amused.

"Have a good day, Lucifer," Morgan replies, turning around without another word.

"King Lucifer, angel. Remember that," Lucifer shouts after him, making Morgan pause. He looks back with a smirk on his lips.

"Of course," Morgan replies, though he does not call him the title like he is meant to. If anything, he sounds as sarcastic as I do. I kinda like it. It makes me smile as Morgan walks away, and Lucifer sees it when I look back at him. His eyes narrow on me for a moment, and fear makes my lips dry as I look at the devil himself getting angry.

"Mr. Morganach, do not forget to see me later. I want to hear your story of how you killed another angel, your best friend, if I'm not mistaken. It was gossip even the ears of hell heard." My heart beats so loudly as Morgan tenses and turns his head back, nodding once but his eyes trying to find mine.

He killed an angel. His best friend? *Why the fuck would he do that?* Maybe Mr. Morganach isn't the good guy, but sure as fuck, the fallen angel I'm in the room with is no better. Lucifer slams the door shut and walks past me down the corridor, leaving me nothing to do but follow him, trying to put thoughts of Morgan in the back of my mind. I can ask him about it all later. I pause when I see Lucifer's back and the two long scars where wings must have once been. Almost like he senses me looking, he stops by the door and turns back to me.

"There is a price for being fallen," he tells me, almost sounding human with real emotions until I see his eyes. How I ever thought they were handsome, I don't know.

I see nothing but empty pits of darkness now. Empty and cold. Just like his soul that clearly was the price as much as his wings were. It makes me wonder who ripped them out or if they just fell off. "Wait for me in the living room. I am going to dress." I don't reply, keeping my eyes on his shoulders as he walks through a door and leaves it open for me to follow. I clasp my clammy hands together as I walk into the large dome-shaped room. It is pretty similar to the room I have, the same style kitchen on the one side and the same sofas facing a glass wall. I walk to the glass, looking out at the almost calm sea. How can it be so calm when my emotions are anything but?

I think this is the most still I have ever seen the sea since I came to the academy, though rain still falls down on us. I look down and regret it the moment I do. Standing on the edge of the cliff are four Hellers and a pile of bodies. Some wolves, some who did not shift, and each one of the bodies is smothered in blood. The Hellers pick body after body up and throw them into the sea, like they are nothing more than a fish that escaped the water. I gasp as sickness fills my throat, and I turn around, rushing to the kitchen sink before throwing up. Not much comes up as I shakily turn on the tap and slide down to the floor, wrapping my arms around my legs and pressing my forehead into them, wishing I could erase this whole evil fucking academy.

"Alexandria, how depressing it is to see you like this," Lucifer states as he squats down in front of me.

"You killed them all for fucking sport, and I'm depressing!" I scream at him as I raise my head and meet his green eyes that are the perfect shade of moss. They remind me so much of Morgan's eyes, but there is a big, big difference. I see nothing good in Lucifer's eyes, nothing but cold contempt for the world he sees as his.

"Death is a blessing for creatures like them. Don't you see that?" he asks me, tilting his head to the side like I'm an interesting creature. He holds a hand out, and he has to be fucking crazy if he thinks I'm going to take it. After a long pause, he seems to finally get the memo and crosses his arms as he stands up. "Fine, if it pleases you, I promise not to harm another wolf in this academy until we leave."

"Leave?" I ask.

"When we are mated, we will not live here. I do detest this place," he remarks so casually. "I want your demon to appear, and being around me as well as going to hell will give her more power. She is my mate after all."

"I'm not ever going to be your mate, Lucifer," I spit out, feeling a sharp pain in my head as he goes blurry for a second.

"Ah, I see your demon is closer than I thought," Lucifer comments. "We will not be waiting for your eighteenth birthday or going to hell after all. You are stronger than expected."

"Fuck you," I bite out as I shake my head, the pain disappearing.

"And call me Luc. We are friends, no?" he asks with a laugh.

"No!" What is flipping wrong with this guy? "We are not friends. We are nothing other than one guy who thinks he owns someone that hates him."

"Tut, tut, Alexandria. I don't think I own you;

I know I do," he replies, and an almost sweet sounding laugh escapes his lips. "Now, stand up, and we will talk about the next few weeks. Including your parents' trial."

"What?" I scramble to my feet at the mere mention of my parents' trial, and he damn well knows he has me as I follow him into the living room. He waves a hand at the only chair in the room as he sits on the sofa and spreads his legs and crosses his arms. His eyes drift up my dress, from my legs to my chest. Every second of it makes me extremely uncomfortable, and I have to restrain my urge to hit him with something. His eyes fix on my chest, and before I can tell him he is a rude bastard, he begins talking.

"That necklace, why do you wear it? Do you not want your demon to be free?" he asks me. "I wondered what stopped the change back then; I see what it is now."

"It's just a gift from my uncle," I reply, lifting it up with one hand. "What do you mean?"

"You know nothing. It is really very annoying," he replies and shakes his head. "I have decided I do not wish to interrupt your tutoring here, but in the next month, there are many events I wish you to attend at my side. It will give us time to bond, and when I don't need you, you may carry on with your tutoring."

"What events?" I question.

"Your parents' trial, for example," he says, and I struggle to keep my excitement and nerves about that one under wraps.

"You could free them tomorrow if you wanted to be my friend," I say.

"I could, but I won't. They took five souls from me, souls that are meant to belong to me, and they are gone. I want to know how they did that," he muses, and I grit my teeth. Bastard. "We must spend a week at the wolves' pack. I want a new agreement, and they are celebrating. It will be fun for us to attend."

"What could they be celebrating after you killed all the wolves here?" I ask.

"They don't see the wolves here as their pack members. Their souls, their bodies, their everything belongs to me from the moment they are sent here to serve," he replies, talking about the dead wolves like they are nothing.

I hate it.

"The funny thing about belonging to someone is that you have to choose them first," I reply. "And I know not one of their souls ever would have chosen you to serve."

"Not if you are born to a debt, Alexandria," he tells me. "And only I can release them from that debt. No one else, especially not your lower-class demon parents. We will find out the truth, one way or another. The trial is my way of respecting you, Alexandria. If they were anyone else, I would drag them to hell and torture them to find out the truth."

"If this is your idea of respect, it is sorely lacking in many areas, Lucifer," I reply.

"Maybe you are not as stupid as I thought you once were," he moves so quickly off the sofa and is in front of me in the next second, his large arms boxing me into the chair. He grabs the necklace off my neck, and it snaps, hurting the back of my neck as he takes it. "Though you are stupid to have kept this on as long as you did. I want your demon to come out to play, and you can't have this on to do that." I flinch as he finally moves away and slides the necklace into his trouser pocket.

"Can I leave?" I ask, not liking him so close to me.

"Of course, Alexandria," he says. If he is

trying to put me at ease, it isn't working. I stand up and quickly walk to the door, but he stops me. Of course it wasn't that easy. "One more thing."

"Yes?" I ask, reaching out and gripping the door as I turn my head back.

"If you try to disobey me. If you touch any other male in a way I don't like, I will make sure your parents lose the trial, and I will take them to hell to find my answers. Their freedom rests solely on your shoulders, Alexandria. I suggest you do as you are told."

"Do threats always work for you, Lucifer?" I ask.

"Yes, because I *always* act on them. Don't test me, I do not wish to see you cry over your parents' dead bodies." I grit my teeth so hard that it hurts as I walk through the door and pull it shut behind me.

Fuck.

## CHAPTER
# THREE

THE DEMON HAS COME OUT TO PLAY

"Who the hell are you?" I ask the Heller in my apartment when I shut the door, seeing him in the kitchen...cooking some bacon by the smell of it. His sword is resting on the counter, his hood still covers his face, and I wonder if the material is fireproof. They look like the grim reaper, and it's a weird thing to see one of them cooking bacon.

"Your personal Heller for protection and any other services you may wish. I will stay in the slave room as there are no more wolf slaves in the academy for the time being," he says so neutrally, so closed off that it makes me more irritated than ever before. My skin itches, my hands curl into fists as pain sparks inside my head.

*Killing the fool who entered our home would be so easy for us,* my demon suggests, her voice is happy and excited at the prospect of murder. No surprise there though.

"Don't be mad at him, he is cooking me bacon," Amethyst says, running into the room and jumping on the counter. "Where have you been? I am starving." I ignore Amethyst altogether as I keep my eyes on the Heller while he slides the bacon onto a plate and hands it to Amethyst. She pauses before eating, looking directly at me with her bright purple eyes. "Okay, I'm happy. Now you can get rid of him."

"So Hellers are replacements for the wolves that were murdered here?" I ask the Heller. "In fact, I don't even care. Get out of my room."

"I don't have to be told twice," Amethyst says, running out of the room looking very freaked out. *What the Heller is wrong with her?*

"Miss Cameron, I am entrusted by his highness to—" he sputters at the end of his sentence, his eyes widening in fear as he reaches for his sword, pressing his back against the counter. I can hardly focus on him as anger is making everything blurry, and the pain in my head is rising ever so slowly.

"I said get the fuck out!" I shout, but my voice doesn't sound like me at all. I cry out as I fall to my knees, hearing the Heller running out the door in the distance, but I can't focus on anything but the searing pain in my head as the floor and my hands go blurry in front of me. My heart pounds so loudly in my ear, blocking out all the sounds of the world, and I struggle to breathe, feeling a stabbing feeling in my heart. A part of me just wants to give up, to give into the pain and warmth slowly taking me. I have no one at my side, my death would make everything happy and light again. I'm nothing but a threat to the world. I'm nothing to anyone.

"Lex, look at me!" I hear a voice I know through the haze, a voice that calls to me more than I ever thought anyone could. One I trust... even when I shouldn't. Warm hands rest on my shoulders, but I can't reply. The warmth of his hands makes the world seem real once again. It feels like he is holding me back from death, not letting me go. I want to go. I want to slip away into nothing, where there is no pain.

*Where there is no heartbreak.*

"Don't you dare give up on me, Alexandria Cameron! There is nowhere your soul can go that I won't follow. Don't you dare give up!" The voice shouts at me, demanding I give in to his commands, making me want to fight away the darkness that lulls me. I can't speak as my head shoots up, meeting the gaze of Nikoli, who doesn't exactly look like Nikoli right now. His black hair now has two horns circling out of it, pointing up into the sky, and his eyes have lost the purple touch they once had; now they are all green.

Like Lucifer's eyes but so, so much more beautiful and enchanting.

Nikoli covers my hand with his, and I watch the movement, noticing how his fingers are black with long sharp nails, and as he lifts my hand, I see mine are just the same.

"Hello. I've wanted to meet you for a long time. Are you like Lexi?" Nikoli asks, his gaze set on mine, his voice the same as the Nikoli I always have known. They are one in the same, his demon and him.

Working together.

That isn't the same for me right now, I don't have any control, and I know my demon has no interest in giving me control back. It makes me wish my parents were here to guide and help me through this, or any family for that matter.

A weak part of me is thrilled it is Nikoli with me, a part of me that still sees Nikoli as my own.

"She is weak," a voice speaks out of my lips, a dark, seductive voice of a woman that is not me. "She wanted to give up her life, let the darkness take her with no fight." I feel guilty for a second as Nikoli looks angry and lost for words. I should have fought, I should have never thought giving up was the right thing to do.

"Weak is a word more fitting for someone who does not want to fight. Lexi is fighting for what she believes in, so how can she be weak?" he eventually asks. "Lexi might have had a short moment of doubt, but it was brief and gone. She fought for her life." My body moves on its own accord, my demon doing it all as we stand up and away from Nikoli. My demon doesn't trust him, not like I do.

"Why do you still stand here?" she asks, tilting her head to the side. "We are not yours." That makes him angry; it makes him frown and almost glare in response.

"You should talk with Lexi and make a

connection. I see in your eyes that you are stronger than anyone could know and that you mean me no harm," he warns, stepping closer, and we watch every single movement. And we are not impressed.

"Do. Not. Tell. Me. What. To. Do." The voice is so cold as it responds, and in one swift movement, my body jumps up and kicks Nikoli hard in the chest, and he spins through the air, smashing into the glass and flying out of it to the cliff.

"Nick!" I shout in my head, fear making everything seem so much worse.

"Can you hear me?" I ask, but no real sound leaves my lips. It's just me speaking to me in my head.

Which is all kinds of fucked up.

"Of course I can. We are connected," my voice says, speaking to herself. She doesn't look once more at the smashed window to see where Nikoli is, but I do try to turn my head that way. It doesn't work, and my lips only laugh as we walk into the bathroom and to the mirror. It's all kinds of weird to see yourself...and not recognise yourself. My brown hair is now black and circled in thick locks around my shoulders and down to my stomach. I have two silver horns with beautiful etched swirls and stars all over them. There are black symbols running up my cheeks at the side, and they meet in the middle of my forehead before disappearing into my hairline. My eyes are black, an endless, empty black that makes me want to look away.

"I heard we have to bond for this to work," I tell...myself. My demon. A part of me that has been hidden away, waiting for me to be strong enough to accept her.

"We will," my demon softly replies, kindly almost. "But I will have what I want."

"And what is that?" I ask nervously. If she wants a mass murder or something flipping messed up, this isn't going to end well. Please, *please* say she is saner than she has appeared so far.

"A throne," she whispers to me. "My throne in hell, with who I choose at our side to protect us."

"With Lucifer, the crazy fallen angel?" I nervously ask.

"No...he must die," she all but growls. "I will not be challenged by a pretender."

"Oh, well, we are in agreement on the important things then," I say, feeling some relief. I can get on board with her plan.

"If you need me, only say my name," she tells me. "And never wear the necklace. I must be able to protect us both. You are too weak for such things." I try not to take insult at that, but it's not easy.

"What is your name?" I ask, feeling stronger than I ever have before. I'm not alone, I never have been because she has always been here, waiting for me. Supporting me. Whatever happens, I can never truly be alone.

"Dakallan." The name fills my mind as everything goes fuzzy, and I feel myself falling only to be greeted by darkness.

CHAPTER
# FOUR

THE HEART IS AN EASY THING TO BREAK

As I wake up, I hear the soft tune of someone humming, a tune I've never heard before, but I really do like it; it is enchanting as much as it is melodic. It sounds sad, lost almost, as I breathe in the scent of the person I'm being held by.

Claus Lucifer. One of my half demon, half angel guys who left me when I needed them the most. I'm disappointed in Claus as much as I am in Nikoli, but a stronger part of me is just happy to be close to him. I like to think I made them better people, better demons and less destructive than they were when we first met.

I made them human.

And now they aren't even mine anymore.

Their father has taken that from us both. My heart hurts in my chest the more I think about it, the more I realise this might be the last time Claus holds me in his arms. It makes me not want to wake up and instead keep my eyes closed, my breathing heavy so that I can enjoy his embrace a little longer. Just a little longer.

It's strange how I can tell who he is from just how he smells, but the distinct and seductive scent of peppermint and traces of lavender is part of who Claus Lucifer is. I open my tired eyes to see I'm lying on Claus's chest in my bed, his hand stroking my hair ever so gently. The motion is soothing, relaxing me back into a false sense of safety and comfort. I'm still fully clothed, and to my surprise, so is Claus. I guess it's because I'm not his mate anymore. No need to impress me.

"Where did you learn that song? The one you were humming?" I softly ask Claus, wanting to know. It sounds familiar to me, but I'm not sure from where exactly.

"I don't know. I've always had it in my head since I was a child. It's a haunting melody, huh?" he enquires. I only nod as I sit up, my brown hair falling around my shoulders, and he looks at me in a way a friend should not. His eyes burn with desire and want, mimicking my own feelings. "You will be happy to know we got all the wolves out, the ones who were still alive that is. That was what Nikoli came to tell you this morning, but he found you turning into your demon. It's impressive that you are doing so well."

"Is Nikoli alright?" I ask as everything rushes back to me, and Claus's lips pull up in a grin as he sits up.

"Other than his ego being sorely damaged beyond repair, he is fine," he tells me, and I sigh, nodding, knowing I need to make it up to him somehow.

"I didn't mean to...well, she might have wanted to hurt Nikoli, but I didn't have control—" I pause as he rests a finger against my lips.

"It's normal for your demon to be aggressive when it is new. It's like an animal being locked in, caged its whole life, and it's suddenly let free. I'm surprised you both have an understanding already. I was in a coma state for two weeks until my demon gave me control back," he admits to be, rubbing the back of his neck, clearly wishing he could forget that time.

"I'm sorry, but what is a coma state?" I question.

"When your demon takes over and you have no control. They can only do it without your permission at the start, and then you will become one. Your strength will be like hers when you want it to," he explains to me. We are both silent and tense for a long moment.

"Right. Claus..." I start to change the subject to the elephant in the room.

"Want to talk about how you are apparently my dad's mate?" he asks.

"I don't belong to him," I reply. "I never, ever will. I'd rather die, to be quite honest."

"You do, and you can't belong to us anymore," he says, climbing out of the bed and walking to my bedroom door. "It's best you accept your fate like all of us have to."

"Wait," I call him, and he pauses, his back tense. "Do you want me to belong to you?"

"More than anything I've ever wanted in my life," he softly says, though he doesn't look at me. "But what we want is not what we can get. My dad would kill me in an instant and kill anyone who comes near you. I will always protect you, Lexi. Always. Even if it means never being anything more than a stranger to you. I came here to say goodbye. A real goodbye."

"I don't want to say goodbye, Claus!" I shout at him, sliding off the bed and standing up. "Look at me, please."

"You are not mine, and I am not yours, Lexi! You need to accept this shit and let me go!" he shouts at me, and I stumble back, feeling like he just stabbed me a few times in my heart. He has given up.

"You should leave then...and please don't make this harder by coming back. Tell Nikoli the same," I just about manage to say, my voice cracking with the emotions I'm holding back.

"Nikoli isn't smart, and he won't stay away," Claus comments, taking another step forward, almost looking regretful as he looks back once. "I fucking wish I wasn't smart too." I stay silent as he walks away from me and out of my apartment. I rub my chest from the sharp, dull pain I feel there as I wipe away tears.

I didn't want them as my mates anyway; at least that's what I tell myself, because the truth hurts way too much.

*Why the hell should I care?* Why shouldn't I just move on? I shake my head as my tummy rumbles, and I try to think back to the last time I ate. I can't even remember. I slide out of bed and walk to the door just as I hear a familiar voice.

"I have not been fed in hours since you passed out," Amethyst grumbles, and I walk around the corridor to see her sitting on the counter near where Sera kept the packets of food.

"I'm sorry. It's been a long day, Amethyst," I tell her, expecting her to be the judgemental little cow she usually is, but instead she walks to me and rests her head on my chest. I pick her up and hug her as all the emotions I've been holding in burst out in a wave, and I can't stop the tears as sobs leave my lips. I sink down onto the floor, holding Amethyst to me as I try to calm down, and she purrs softly.

"Don't let anything beat you down, Lexi. You are a goddess in a dark world, and you are just starting to be who you need to be," she tells me, sounding old and wise way beyond her years.

"What self-help books have you been reading?" I chuckle around a sob, wiping my cheeks with the side of my hand.

"All of them. I believe in the art of meditation to soothe the soul," she remarks.

"My soul needs more than soothing, Amethyst. I don't know what to do, and all I want to do is run to my parents and have them tell me what to do," I admit. I need my mum to hug me and tell me the twins are stupid idiots, and then for my dad to suggest ways to make them pay, while making me laugh.

They always fixed everything, and I feel like I'm constantly free falling through life since I got here and they aren't here to catch me.

"It's normal for a bird to be scared of falling off the nest. Only when you fall do you learn how to fly," she tells me, rubbing her head against my chin to lift it up.

"Actually, that is pretty good advice...you know, from a cat," I say.

"I'm a smart cat," she purrs.

"That you are," I say, lifting her up in my arms and looking into her purple eyes. What would I do without my talking cat?

# CHAPTER
# FIVE

SOMEONE NEEDS COFFEE IN THE MORNING

"You didn't come to training," Morgan snaps as I walk out of my room, and he nearly makes me jump out of my skin. Has no one ever told him shouting at people when they walk out of their apartment is rude? "I thought something fucking happened to you." I take a deep breath and close the door, turning to face my grumpy angel.

"I got a note saying I have to come to The Choosing class half an hour early and that I was to miss training. I can get the note if you want it," I say. "Trust me, I'd rather be in training with you." Which is true. I've grown to like my time alone with Morgan and his teasing and just everything about him.

I'm getting obsessed with my teacher, and I have no intention of stopping. I'm thinking he is just as obsessed with me. At least I'm hoping. Though he hasn't kissed me or said anything to make me think he likes me since the ball. Maybe his feelings have changed? I just can't tell with Morgan anymore. He is so possessive and protective, but that is his nature.

"No. Let's just go," he grumbles, not waiting as he storms off down the corridor and past the statue.

"Do you drink coffee in the morning? I'm just thinking it might make you more of a morning person than you currently are," I say when I jog to his side, my arm brushing against his. I *almost* stop in my tracks from the tiny amount of contact.

"I don't drink coffee. Water is better for you," he sourly replies as we pass three students, all of whom bow their heads at me and nervously move out of the way.

"No wonder you are so moody," I remark.

"You're a pain in my ass, Miss Cameron," he replies with a bit of snark in his tone. It's playful though and teasing.

"But you like it, Mr. Morganach," I smoothly

reply, flirting just a little, and he shakes his head, even though I see the little turn up of his lips. I nearly scream as he quickly pulls me into a closet we pass and shuts the door behind me. Before I can even ask what he is doing, he kisses me.

Holy shit, *Morgan* is kissing me. I lean into him as he gently parts my lips, softly applying pressure as he presses me into the wall, his hard body pushed against mine. Every soft brush of his lips makes me want more, lures me into him like a siren singing to the sea. Just as I slide my hands up his neck, he pulls back, his face hidden in the shadows. I almost flipping whimper. *Whimper.* That's what he has brought me to.

"I wasn't planning to do that. You are too addictive, Alexandria," he mutters, sounding more frustrated and lust driven than I expected. It wasn't just me that felt that then. The draw between us, the almost bond tugging us together. It felt right and natural to kiss him; it felt like something I've always been looking for.

"I, err, wasn't planning to kiss you back either. But I'm totally happy to do that again," I suggest, and I can almost see the amusement in his eyes, even in the dark closet that smells of bleach and dust. It reminds me of a dusty closet I was in once as a kid...but why was I in a closet?

"We will talk about this later, but I did need to tell you something in private today," he says, placing his hands on the wall on either side of my head and leaning in closer. We both breathlessly stare at each other, neither one of us moving until I go to lean forward, but a broom falls off the wall, whacking Morgan in the arm, and we both jump away from each other. I don't know who laughs first, but the next second we are both laughing as Morgan picks the broom up. He has a deep laugh, one I never expected to love as much as I do. I'm sad when we both stop, and I remember what he even said in the first place.

"What is it you need to tell me?" I ask.

"Do you remember the professor I told you about, the one I want you to see about our secret?" he quietly asks, not actually saying the words "angel blessed" in case someone is listening in. So far, it is our little secret. Our deadly secret, because if anyone found out, there would be trouble.

"Yes, I remember," I reply.

"We go tonight," he informs me.

"Go where?" I question with a frown.

"To the Angel Academy where he works, of course. I have made plans, be ready at midnight," he tells me, and without a reply, he walks out the closet, leaving me alone in here. I wait a few seconds, my fingers resting on my lips, knowing I'm never going to forget that kiss, before leaving the closet and walking into the crowd of students like nothing happened at all.

I KNOCK on the closed classroom door before going inside, where Lucifer and Mr. Johan are leaning against the desk, laughing like they are college roommates who are just reunited. Instead of the real truth. The King of Hell's laugh is not as scary as it damn well should be, not to me anyway. He turns to me as I pull the door shut and cross my arms, waiting for them to say something.

"I remember that time well, old friend. I wish for you to come back to hell soon and we can test our theory on the dawn pixies," Lucifer says, and they both laugh once more. Mr. Johan finally seems to get some sense and leans forward, bowing his head before looking towards me.

"Miss Cameron, it is good to see you as always. As The Choosing class is a preparational class for choosing a future, I'm afraid it is no use to you. The stone has already chosen you as its queen," he reminds me.

"So this lesson will be our time. There is much you do not know of hell, heaven and earth. I will be playing teacher, considering Mr. Johan tells me how much you seem to like your teachers," Lucifer states, and I feel like my lips are burning with Mr Morganach's kiss. He can't know that. It was our secret.

"The teachers here are different than any I have had before," I comment, leaving out how nearly all of them are bat shit crazy and deadlier than anything I've ever known. There is one teacher that is different, but as he told me once, he is a fucking bad teacher.

"So am I. Now sit if you will," Lucifer asks, waving a hand at the desk. Mr. Johan bows his head at me as he passes and leaves the room. I sit in the desk, crossing my arms again as my demon ever so gently presses into my mind. Lucifer's calm collected image suddenly changes into one of deep interest, but then my demon vanishes once more, and he clears his throat.

"I brought you something. A gift unlike any other," Lucifer comments. I don't want his fucking gift, but for my parents' and my own sake, I tightly smile as he picks a red leather-bound book up off the desk and slides it in front of me. There is nothing but smooth red leather on the outside, and I run my fingers over it, going to open the inside. "Wait. What this book shows you is my past. My truth. I wish for you to see it all and judge it for yourself."

"Why would you show me this?" I ask.

"Because I want you to see my plan. Our plan, one that has been around for thousands of years," he explains. "But it will take time for you to see everything."

"And what plan is that?" I ask.

"The plan of how we will become king and queen of them all," he tells me, before pulling the book open, and red light flashes into my eyes, so brightly it stings. When I open my eyes, I'm not in the classroom anymore, instead I'm stood in a library. It's a massive dome, filled with thousands of books held in pure silver bookcases. The floor itself is silver as I stand on it, and four spheres of fire burn in the middle of the room, constantly spinning and casting light into every inch of the room. The doors behind me slam open, and two angels walk in, both with long white wings that are so bright it's hard to look away. They wear white cloaks with hoods covering their faces, and they stop in the centre of the room as the doors close themselves.

"Did you hear the song of the poet?" the one angel asks. His voice sounds young and innocent, though the accent is very foreign to me.

"Aye, I did. The wee lass has nought but stories in her head," the other man replies, not leaving where he came from to the imagination. The thick Scottish accent is hard to understand for a brief moment. Even though I lived in Scotland myself, I still could never understand any of the people who live north of Inverness, where I'm sure the land itself makes their accent impossible to understand.

"It was not a story, but a prophecy. I feel it will be," the other replies.

"Enough of this, Lucifer. We must get back to the lass; we are charged with her care," the other replies, and I realise this must have been Lucifer when he was younger, before he fell into hell.

They both turn back and walk to the doors, and I run after them, sliding through the door before it closes. I don't look much at the corridor as they go into the room opposite, and I head inside before that door leaves me out.

This room is plain but somehow grand with its silver touches here and there. Silver vines wrap around the pillars of a wooden bed, where a fragile woman lies, shaking ever so gently. Lucifer and the other angel simply watch her for a long time before she suddenly sits up, her eyes glowing blue, a bright blue that reminds me of the blue sapphire necklace my mom wears that, when the light hits the necklace, almost seems to glow.

"Leave us and get Master Adro," Lucifer demands, and the other angel runs past me as Lucifer moves to sit on the bed, lowering his hood for the first time. His hair is longer here, in waves around his face, but it is the same white colour. He looks so young, so innocent as he stares at the woman. She quickly turns to him and cups his cheeks with her hands, speaking so fast I barely hear it.

*"Lucifer, you will love only one.*
*Her soul is bound to no gods, to no one.*
*Four will run like horses at her side.*
*One for war.*
*One for love.*
*One for power,*
*And one for truth.*
*Love is endless and meant not for you.*
*Fall once, and forever you shall fall.*
*Hell awaits those who seek what they should not.*
*Heaven is the curse of which you will never escape.*
*All that begins here must end in the same light.*
*Forever may she reign...forever may you fall."*

THE WOMAN SHAKES EVER SO SLIGHTLY before she collapses back, and white smoke fills the room, replacing it with the classroom as Lucifer pulls the book away.

"Was the prophecy about Lilith? The twins' mother?" I ask him as I try to breathe normally, and my hands shake ever so much under the table.

"I thought it was, many, many years ago," he says, glowering, "but she was a pretender."

"And now?" I ask.

"I want it to be another," he replies, staring at me like he is crazy enough to think that I'm anything to do with that prophecy.

"I'm not —"

"I don't expect you to agree with the words of the prophecy, but they are what they are. Have you ever heard of the four horsemen of the apocalypse?" he asks me, and I'm gathering he is referring to the "four will run like horses at her side" part of the prophecy. That fairy tale can't be real...can it?

"The story, yes..." I muse.

"When a new queen rises, so will the four who ride at her side through the pathway of hell. I will be the king at your side, and I'm sure you will find your four riders at some point in your life. It all fits together, everything I have ever waited for since the day I just showed you. It's all happening, and you will make me so happy, Alexandria," he says with a big smile that I'm sure he wants me to return. Only, slight issue...I don't want to return it in any way at all.

"No," I say, and his smile drops into a thin line, his eyes going from happy to flipping mad.

"Do I have to remind you that your parents' first hearing is in two weeks?" he asks.

"No," I bite out.

"Good. Tomorrow we are going on a trip for a week, to the wolves I told you of. Then you can resume normal classes until the trial," he states, crossing his arms and daring me to challenge him.

"Sounds perfectly planned out," I sourly reply, the idea of a trip away with Lucifer leaving that sour taste in my mouth.

"Oh it is. Class dismissed," Lucifer states, clapping his hands together like the crazy fucker he really is. I watch him walk to the door, hoping he won't say another word, but of course he does as he opens the door. "One more thing, do not bring your cat with you to the wolves."

"Why?" I ask.

"I don't like cats," he snaps rather angrily before slamming the door shut behind him. I rest my forehead on the desk for a moment, sucking in a deep breath. I only have to pretend until my parents are free, then they will get me the hell out of this mess.

Or I will save myself and them to boot.

# CHAPTER
# SIX

JEALOUSY IS A CRUEL MISTRESS

"Good to see you in class, your highness," Lela's sarcasm is thick as I sit down next to her in Hexing class and drop my spell book onto the table. The room is empty, and we are the only ones in here as I glare at her.

"Drop that shit, I'm just Lexi, and Lucifer is wrong," I mutter.

"I'd jump at being the Queen of Hell if I was you. So much power and respect. Also, Lucifer is hot as fuck, and I don't even like boys," she replies. "Then again, his sons are better, and you love them."

"It's complicated," I say.

"Complicatedly fucked up, sure," Lela

replies, and I shake my head at her as Maggie walks into the classroom, followed by three more students who all sit down. Maggie chooses to sit right in front of me, leaving me a view of her heavy blonde hair and how not a single bit is frizzy or out of place. Lela rolls her eyes at me as I sit back and cross my arms, watching all the students come in and hearing their whispers as they look directly at me. The final student to come in the room is none other than Claus, strutting in like he owns the place. I smile at him as he looks at me, but he doesn't smile back. He moves to sit right next to Maggie, in front of Lela and me as Mrs. Herman comes into the classroom, shutting the door behind her.

"As usual, we will be drawing a new hex symbol for the first half of the lesson, and the second half, I expect you to successfully use the hex symbol," she says before getting a pen and starting to draw the new symbol I haven't seen before on the white board.

"So, Claus, I've heard you're single," Maggie says with a sickeningly sweet voice.

"I've always been single, Maggie," he simply replies, not exactly flirting like she is, but not pushing her away like I want him to. My hand tightens on my pen, so tight I know it's going to burst, as all I see is red. Maggie places her hand on his shoulder and leans into him.

"They aren't worth it," Lela harshly whispers to me, placing her hand over my arm, but I shrug her away as Maggie giggles at something Claus said.

"Dakallan," I say under my breath.

"Oh fuck," I hear Lela say as my demon takes over, and I feel my appearance change. I don't need to talk to my demon to know we are on the same page, and she lets me have control as I reach out and grab Maggie's hair, and I fling her across the classroom as she screams.

"Alexandria! What the fuck are you doing?!" Claus shouts at me, and I sneer at him as I face him.

"You betrayed us, and she is nothing more than bait."

"I'm not yours, Lexi. You can't—"

"You will never tell me what do, because you are a coward, Claus Lucifer."

"I am not," he growls at me, his eyes slowly losing the purple wave and being replaced with green. Claus shakes his head, stopping the change, and he walks over to Maggie, helping her stand up. The anger soon turns to pain as I watch him comfort her, and my demon doesn't need to say a word as we both head for the door.

"You can leave, Miss Cameron. Jealousy is a sin, one we must all learn to cope with," Mrs. Herman quietly tells me as my appearance changes back, and I don't look back as I head out of the door.

*He is ours.*

"No, he is not. We deserve better," I tell my demon, knowing it is true. I will never have a mate who believes running away from me is going to make things better for everyone.

I will never have someone in my life who can hurt me and walk away.

# CHAPTER
# SEVEN

DEATH BY A FLYING HORSE

I never really understood why people pace when they are anxious. It always seemed like a waste of energy and did little more than wear down your shoes. But as I pace, looking at the clock on the wall near the door every minute, I now understand it. It's hard to stay still when you wait for someone or something that makes you nervous.

It's near impossible too. I glance at the fresh glass window that someone fixed when I was out today. The panel Javier used to sneak through is gone...and so are Javier and Sera. I have no doubt that Javier will keep Sera safe, and himself at the same time.

It doesn't help me, not when I miss them

both. I rub the scratch mark on my arm that looks stranger these days than ever before. I lift my sleeve and look at the three lines on the inside of my arm and how the cut almost looks like lines of shining silver. It's not like any cut I've ever had, and I wish Sera would have told me the truth about why she was so scared of it. Why I caught her staring at my arm, lost deep in thought and in fear that I saw dancing across her eyes.

What is wolf marked anyhow? I need to ask someone before I go with Lucifer to the pack tomorrow. Luckily, I know just the angel to ask.

I nearly jump out of my skin when someone knocks the door three times, and I run over, pulling it open to let Morgan in. He wears a thick black cloak, the hood lowered and his wings almost blending into the cloak. In his arms, he has another cloak which he holds up as I shut the door.

"You need to wear this, just in case someone sees us," he explains. "And it might be cold."

"Alright," I say, turning around and lifting my hair as he places the cloak on my shoulders before letting it fall. I slide my arms through the gaps as he walks around and does the top three buttons up for me before meeting my eyes. Ever so gently, he reaches up and tucks a strand of my hair away from my cheek and behind my ear, and I close my eyes as his finger rests on my cheek, enjoying the unassuming happiness of his touch. He steps closer, just leaving a breath of space between us as I open my eyes, finding his in an instant.

"What are you doing to me, Miss Cameron?" he softly asks, sounding nothing like the moody asshole I've come to know.

"The same thing you are doing to me, Mr. Morganach," I breathlessly reply, feeling like all the air in the world has just left me. He leans closer, very carefully brushing his lips against mine as his hands pull my hood up, and he steps away, leaving me in a desperate state of wanting much more than what he gave me.

"We need to leave; we only have a certain time allowance to get in and out of the academy," he tells me, pulling up his own hood and walking to the door. Jogging after him, we head out of the corridor and past the statue before going around it towards a family room that I know leads to the cliff. It reminds me of the time not so long ago that a student tried to kill me, and instead, Morgan killed her.

It reminds me that Morgan is not all good like I see him as sometimes. It reminds me of what Lucifer said about him killing his best friend and how much I need to know the truth behind it.

"Morgan," I whisper, grabbing his arm to stop him in the middle of the room. He looks back, though I can't see his face under the hood.

"What is it?" he sternly asks.

"I need to know something before I go with you," I tell him, letting his arm go and crossing my arms as I take a deep breath. "Was Lucifer telling the truth about you? Did you kill an angel? Your best friend?"

"You want to know the truth, why exactly?" he asks, walking towards me, anger dripping from every word. "Will it make you feel better? Will it make you want me more to know the truth? Or is it that you suddenly don't trust me because of my past? I've never once lied to you and pretended to be innocent, Miss Cameron. You know who I am, and I have nothing to prove."

"Would it make me trust you more to know

your past?" I ask. "The part you are clearly so defensive about."

"No. It fucking wouldn't," he snaps.

"Tell me anyway," I suggest, stepping closer.

"Why?" he demands.

"Because I have feelings for you, and I want to know you. I want to understand everything, Morgan," I reply, being truthful even though putting my feelings out there is risking everything.

"Those feelings are going to get you killed, Miss Cameron," he tensely tells me. "You would be better off thinking and feeling like I am no one."

"My name is Alexandria Cameron, and I'm not no one to you!" I shout at him, losing my temper, and he loses all control right there with me. We crash into each other, our lips finding each other's like there was never any space to begin with. He kisses me like I have always been his, and in this moment, I never want to be anyone else's.

In this moment, there is only Morgan and me. His lips and tongue explore my mouth as he picks me up and cups my ass before pushing my back into the wall. I feel how hard he is as he pushes himself into me more, deepening the kiss, and a spark of pleasure starts to build from the friction. Before that spark can be anything more, he pulls his lips away, and we both breathlessly stare at each other, the moonlight shining on Morgan's back so brightly it looks like his wings are lit up with a thousand stars.

"You are not no one. You could never be that, Alexandria," he tells me, "no matter how much I wish you were for your own safety. Demons and angels aren't destined to be together."

"I don't give a fuck about destiny, Morgan. I only know I care about you, and that isn't going to change," I say, and he smirks, making me smile back at him. I run my hand down his cheek, and he leans into my touch ever so slightly. "Tell me. I won't run from you, I won't see you as less. I know you, Morgan."

"No, you don't and you can't. What Lucifer said was true. I once killed my best friend, and I'm a fucking monster that belongs here," he spits out every word, trying to push me away as he lets me go and turns around. I gulp and step closer, touching the feathers of his wings ever so softly.

"Tell me the rest of the story," I plead with him.

"You don't need the rest of the story to see who I am," he tells me.

"I do," I say quietly. It's a barrier between us, a wall he isn't willing to bring down, and we have enough barriers between us as it is. I need to be closer to him, to find out this part of his past.

"We must go, Miss Cameron." He snaps his emotions shut as harshly as he speaks to me, and blocks me out so quickly that I can hardly keep up as he walks out onto the cliff after opening the door. I try to swallow my disappointment as I follow him out, only to be shocked into silence at the sight of a horse standing on the cliff. The horse is massive, like as big as a truck my dad had once and crashed in the snow. The more shocking thing is the horse has long black wings that rest at its side. The horse is completely covered in silky black fur that the moonlight reflects off as it is that smooth. It has a long mane, braided dozens of times, and there are five silver bands holding the braids together. Morgan rests his hand on the horse's head, closing his eyes ever so slightly before opening them and pulling up his hood as he turns to me.

"Who is this?" I ask.

"Angels ride not only with their wings, but a gift of the gods. This is my familiar of sorts, Neriffe. Every angel is blessed with a horse of their choosing at the start of their first term at The Angel Academy," he explains to me as I get to his side. "It also makes it much easier to travel. Neriffe can fly more quickly than I can."

"To The Angel Academy? On a flying horse?" I mutter, feeling all kinds of nervous. "Maybe we should just forget about all this and—"

"Are you scared of horses?" he asks with a dark grin.

"Not normal, non-flying horses," I reply.

"Have you ever ridden a horse?" he asks.

"No, we have cars. Much safer," I comment, and he shakes his head at me. "Wait, when did you become an angel? How old are you? Did they have cars when you were human?"

"I'm twenty-three years old. Including my human life," he explains to me.

"Oh good, I got worried I kissed an old man or something for a second there," I mumble. "Actually what are the jobs of angels, what do they train you to do with your flying horse? I can't even imagine—"

"Do you ever stop talking when you're nervous?" he interrupts me, clearly amused.

"Unless you have a car door to knock me out with, nope," I say, making him grin as well as frown in the same second. It's rather cute. In a swift motion, Morgan grabs my waist from behind and flies us onto the horse, where I nearly fall off as I try to hold onto Morgan's arms around me for dear life. He grabs the reins at the same time he wraps an arm around my belly and pushes me down with his chest. I rather like being this close to Morgan but not on a horse.

"Keep your head down, or it will hurt your neck," Morgan warns me but with no real explanation to *what* might hurt me.

"What do you mean—" I scream the end of the sentence as Neriffe moves quicker than anything and runs right off the cliff with her wings spread wide, the harsh air blasting against my body almost instantly, taking the voice right from my lungs.

Death by flying horse. That's a new one to write on someone's headstone. I just hope it won't be mine.

# CHAPTER
# EIGHT

THE ANGELS HAVE A PRETTY CASTLE;
HOW IS THAT FAIR?

I don't know how long we are flying at an insane speed before Neriffe suddenly slows, and I gasp in air as I could barely breathe before this point.

"You can look now," Morgan, the asshole who didn't really warn me about this shit, tells me as he straightens up, still keeping an arm around my waist. I open my eyes, blinking a few times at the bright light as Neriffe glides smoothly in the air towards a castle in the clouds. Everything is a blur as I suck in a deep breath and wipe my wet eyes, feeling how cold it is around us. The wind is damn cold up here in the clouds, and the clouds look like silver cotton candy as they surround us. Neriffe smoothly glides in the air, moving slowly and perfectly. Whatever bond Morgan and she have is strong, strong enough that he never once had to guide her as she knew where he wanted to go.

I'm pretty sure Amethyst would have spun around and dropped me off somewhere random. Morgan has the better familiar for sure. I shake my head a little, moving my hair out of my eyes and tucking it behind my ears as we get closer to the castle.

Holy all things in the world, it is the prettiest castle I have ever seen. It's on a massive rock, floating in the middle of dozens of white clouds, and sun shines brightly down onto the castle and small houses around it, and on the beautiful gardens. The castle has what must be dozens of white spiral towers and bridges connecting all of the castle to the main part in the middle. When I look up, wondering how it is day at all in here, I see the sun isn't a sun at all. It's a floating orb of intense light, with angels in a line like a barrier all the way around it.

"Welcome to Neamh, the home of the angels. Never before has a demon set foot here, count yourself lucky," he tells me, turning Neriffe to the side, and I grip his arm that's around me tighter just in case. This is really fucking high up. No matter how beautiful The Angel Academy is, I don't have wings to save me if I fall.

"Are you breaking another rule, Mr. Morganach?" I ask.

"I told you once before, I'm a bad teacher," he replies. I chuckle as I lean back into him, ignoring how being pressed so close to him makes my heart beat faster than how nervous I am being up this high. "Now, hood up, Miss Cameron, there might be angels around even though they should be sleeping." I pull my hood up and hold it in place as Neriffe swoops down, the wind making me catch my breath. Neriffe flies into the nest of pink orchard trees at the back of the castle, gracefully landing on a clearing in the middle of it. Morgan keeps his arm tight around my waist as he flies us up in the air, off Neriffe, and lands us just in front of her.

"One second, I'm going to tie Neriffe up," Morgan tells me, leaving me to go to his horse and take the reins, leading her to a tree before he begins to tie her up. I only hear the flutter of wings before a knife is pressed against my throat, and a large hand grabs my hip, holding me in place.

"Demons aren't allowed to walk the path of grace. Who are you?" the man demands, pushing the dagger hard enough against my neck that it is impossible to reply.

"Let her go before I make you regret it, boy," Morgan's cold voice echoes around my ears. The stillness of the trees, the utter silence makes Morgan look like an angry god. And he is on my side, thank goodness. Morgan walks right up to us, wrapping his hand around the man's hand holding the knife, the one so sharp and close to my throat. For some messed up reason, I feel like Morgan has already saved me, even though he has not.

"She is a demon and—"

"Aye, do as your told and let the lass go this very instant," another voice, a voice much older sounding and familiar to my ears, demands. The knife drops onto the ground near my feet in less than a second, and the hand leaves my hip as I fall into Morgan's waiting arms. He holds me to his side as I turn around and look at the angel on his knees, bowing to the man who just spoke. They both have white wings, so heavenly they are addictive to look at, and they make you just want to touch them. The boy has red hair, curly and bright, but I can't see much else from this angle. I move my gaze to the other man who is the Scottish angel I saw with Lucifer in that book's memories, though he is a lot older now, wrinkles covering his face, and long gray hair that mixes in with the bright white cloak he wears.

"Master Gabriel, it is good to see you after such a time," Morgan says, bowing his head low, but Gabriel doesn't look away from me.

"Aye, we have much to discuss, it seems," Gabriel replies, his tone giving away nothing of his emotions. "As for you, Mr. Georgon, you will go from here and not speak a word of the demon you saw. If you do, aye laddie, you will find out what it is to fly with your wings clipped."

"Y-y-yes," the guy sputters before spreading his large white wings out and shooting off into the sky, splashing soil all over my cloak, which I shake.

"Come, trouble awaits outside," Gabriel states, turning around and walking off out of the trees. Morgan rests his hand on my lower back, ushering me along as we walk out of the trees and through a pretty garden. There are dozens of flowers of all kinds in pots lining the pathway that is filled with little white stones. Every flower, bush and tree we pass is perfect and very healthy. It's clear someone spends a lot of time looking after this place.

We finally come to a trap door on the back of the castle wall, where there is nothing else around. Gabriel rests his hand on the steel door, and it briefly glows white before opening itself, light pouring out from inside. Gabriel walks down the steps, and I follow him into the room, which I suppose must once have been a science lab of sorts. Dozens of strange things are in jars across three shelves around the room, and there are four large desks with strange science equipment on them, tubes going off in every direction.

"Sit, sit, young demon," Gabriel suggests, waving a hand at the chair near him. I look to Morgan who nods, and I know I have to trust Morgan on this guy. I'm here; there's no going back now. I sit in the chair, and Gabriel looks to Morgan, who leans against the desk.

"You said a demon was angel-blessed, but you failed to mention *which* demon was, lad,"

Gabriel says, eyeing me very curiously. "You are the image of your mother, demon."

"I only knew who she was a few days ago. Alexandria didn't even know," he explains. "It is news to us all. News that makes this whole situation more dangerous than we could have known."

"Did your parents not tell you that you are born to be the Queen of Hell, lass?" Gabriel asks.

"My parents know?" I question, and Gabriel clicks his tongue, his eyes holding sadness as he pulls a chair over and places it in front of me before sitting down.

"Let me tell you a story, young Alexandria," he starts off, clasping his hands together in his lap. "Every week on a Sunday, I would go to a church just outside the city of Edinburgh because this church was where I was born, hundreds if not nearly a thousand years ago. I would help the homeless who went there, and give back to the church who looked after me for many years. My mother passed on soon after my birth, and the nuns of Church Augustine brought me up. They were good lasses."

"That's the church me and my family lived in. Is that the one you are talking about?" I ask in surprise. I've read some history of the church in the old books there, and I know it has been around for a very long time and that the nuns did indeed look after young infants left to their care.

"Aye, it is," he tells me. "See, one day two demons came into the church. The very fact they could step onto holy ground proved to me that they were not as evil as most of their kind. Evil actions mark the soul, you see. Demons are not born evil as the world believes; evil has to be chosen. The woman held a small baby, and she begged for my help, for my knowledge of the mark on her baby's thigh...an angel blessing on a demon. Something that should never have existed, because it breaks all the rules we have ever known."

"Me. My parents asked you about me," I fill in.

"You never told me any of this, Gabriel," Morgan interrupts.

"Letters are not safe means of transporting information, lad. Aye, I promised to keep Alexandria's secrets many years ago, and I have never broken a promise," he firmly replies. "Much as I kept your own, lad. If you will remember?"

"What does her mark mean? Will she die and become an angel, if that is even possible?" Morgan asks, changing the subject quickly.

"I've spent nearly eighteen years researching and finding a way this could be at all possible, and it wasn't until this year I found my answer. I'm afraid I owe you an apology, Miss Alexandria," he says, reaching his hand out and placing it on my shoulder.

"Why?" I ask, almost not wanting the answer in case it is bad.

"I came and saw your parents, and it is likely my visit to them that revealed their hiding place," he tells me. "It was foolish, and I am deeply sorry. Your parents are good demons, with souls made of light. They do not deserve the life they have been forced into."

"You weren't the only one there. Lucifer was there before they were captured, he might have given us all away," I gently say. "Either way, you helped my parents, and they clearly trusted you. Do not feel bad for a mistake."

"What did you find out?" Morgan interrupts. "We do not have much time before Alexandria needs to be back at The Demon Academy."

"Nothing good, I'm afraid," he tells me. "I

found a book written before there was an Angel or Demon Academy, before there was anything but rumours of magic in the air. When the earth had just been created by who knows who and humans made wars for the right to own their land. This book should not have existed in such a time, but it's impossibility is not important, only what it foreshadows."

"I saw you once...with Lucifer. You were his friend," I blurt out, needing to see his reaction.

"Are you accusing me of being on the wrong side, Miss Alexandria?" he asks, and I don't answer.

"I trust Gabriel with my life. Whatever past he has with Lucifer, it is the past," Morgan tells me.

"Would it help you, lass, to know the church was my hiding place, one I willingly gave to your parents to keep you safe? I surely am more invested in your safety than one should admit," Gabriel reminds me. "In fact, helping you and your parents breaks every rule in the truce between angels and demons—it could mean war."

"I'm sorry. I don't know who to trust anymore," I admit.

"You made a correct choice in trusting this angel. Of all my students in the many, many years I have taught here at the academy, Morgan is more loyal and braver than them all. I have deep respect for the lad," he tells me. "Always trust him."

"You're going to make me blush, old man," Morgan comments.

"Call me old again, and I will remind you of the time my old butt beat yours in training," Gabriel warns, and Morgan grins, a real smile that is almost playful. It's something rare to see on Morgan's face, and I find myself staring for a moment too long. Long enough for Gabriel to clear his throat, and I quickly look back, schooling my expression. Gabriel is too smart, he saw it. My red cheeks likely don't help matters either.

"What did you find, Gabriel?" Morgan reminds him, the serious tone back.

"There was but one sentence, just one sentence, and I know in my soul, it is a warning only for you, Alexandria," he tells me. "I feel like I am meant to tell you it; it is a higher calling, if you will."

"Tell me, please," I ask.

*"She who walks to death alone, marked with a silver scar and angel blessing, will fall with the world at her feet."*

"What is that meant to mean?" I ask, knowing it means me. The wolf blessing is the silver scar, and I have an angel blessing. But why would I walk to death alone?

"That you must never choose to walk to death, Alexandria. No matter the cost, you must not choose that path. You will lose far, far more than the price you want," he tells me. "Some things are too great for any of us to deal with."

"I don't understand," I admit.

"Understanding comes in time. Greater forces are controlling this story," he tells me. "I wish I could tell you more, but poets, a race of beings who could tell the future, are dead. There is only the past now."

"Well, whoever is writing this story is crazy! Why can't they just write me a happy ending or something simple?" I demand, standing up.

"Alexandria." Morgan gently touches my arm, and I pause, taking a deep breath to calm myself down. I'm scared...more scared than I have ever been at the academy, because I know death is promised to everyone, everywhere. How can I ever escape it? "Wait for me by the door. I won't be long." I shakily nod to him, looking back at Gabriel before I walk away.

"Thank you for helping me now and all those years ago. Thank you for giving me the safe and happy years with my parents that I couldn't have had otherwise," I tell him. "I will always owe you, Gabriel."

"It was an honour to be called to help you, Miss Alexandria. Be blessed and safe in your travels," he replies. I bow my head, feeling like it's the correct thing to do before turning around and walking to the door, resting my back against the stone wall as Morgan talks quietly with Gabriel.

*I can hear them, so should you.* My demon's voice fills my head as suddenly the room amplifies with sound, and their conversation is so loud it's like they are right next to me.

"You should tell her, Morgan. It's unfair she is in the dark," Gabriel warns.

"I will," Morgan replies, and I see him place his hand on Gabriel's shoulder. Gabriel covers it with his own and pats it a few times. "Thank you for all you have done for me. I was a fucked-up mess in this place and worse afterwards. Without your guidance, I would not be here today and found what I have. I owe you debts I'm not sure I will ever be able to pay back."

"Debts are not owed from you to me, lad. I saw great potential in you from the first day we met, and that has not changed to this day. We all have our own destinies, our own stories. So I ask you this, why are you standing here talking to an old man like me when a beautiful woman is waiting for you over there?" I can almost see Morgan's smile as he says goodbye and walks over to me, his hand resting on my back as he opens the door, looking out first before we walk out to the garden.

"Any chance we don't have to fly back home?" I ask.

"Unless you know how to use holy fire to travel already...which I doubt, then yes," he replies.

"Can you teach me how to use holy fire?" I ask.

"That was our next lesson, tomorrow morning," he tells me.

"Lucifer is taking me to the wolf pack tomorrow," I say, and he looks at me with burning anger. "I can't say no; he threatened my parents." A small part of me is happy to go to the pack, just so I can see Javier again. And Sera. I miss them every day. Not that I'm going to tell Javier that. I'm still angry at him; that hasn't changed.

"How long until the trial?" he asks me.

"A week," I tell him.

"Then after the trial, your parents will be safe, and we can get you away from him," he tells me, placing his hand around my hip.

"He thinks I'm his mate, Morgan. There isn't anywhere he won't look," I remind him.

"No problem," Morgan coldly replies. "If he comes after you, I'm going to kill him myself."

I have no doubt Morgan is telling me the truth, but what if he loses? What if the devil can't be killed?

# CHAPTER NINE

## A LONG DRIVE WITH SATAN. HEAVEN SAVE ME PLEASE

Sitting in a limo with the devil is more awkward and uncomfortable than I could have ever imagined. Especially as he just stares at me, making me want to open the limo door and throw myself out into the road. Better that than this long drive with Satan himself dressed in an expensive suit with staring issues.

"Do you ever speak? Or are you mad at me?" he muses, stretching his arms out across the seat as I sit on the other side of the limo, as far away from him as possible.

"You murdered hundreds of wolves. People. You killed people with real emotions and real lives that you took away for nothing more than sport. We will never be friends, Lucifer," I tell him, because it's true. Even if he didn't do that, he is way too late to try and steal my heart. It's already shared between his two sons, both of who are giant assholes, a wolf who literally used me, and an angel who has dark, possibly terrifying secrets.

Lucifer doesn't stand a chance.

"Good thing I do not wish to be your *friend*, Alexandria," he smoothly replies, trying to be charming, I suspect. It doesn't work on me, and from the anger in his gaze, he knows it.

"How long until we arrive?" I ask, getting the feeling it has been at least an hour of driving so far. We are heading far inland, well away from the academy on the edge of the cliff. It's strange to know the island is this big and somehow the rest of the world doesn't know of its existence.

"The pack lands are on the other side of the island, and it will be no longer than another ten minutes until we hit the treeline that marks their border," he tells me. "The angels in the skies above, the demons on a cliff, fairy tales on a tiny island nearby, and wolves hiding in the forest. What fun lands these are!"

"You aren't going to go on a mass killing

spree here, are you?" I question, ignoring his not so funny joke.

"Would you betray me and tell if I said yes?" he asks, leaning forward and clasping his hands together.

"Yes," I automatically answer, and he laughs, which I don't join in.

"So sweetly honest you are, Alexandria. Perhaps we are closer to being true mates than I thought," he says, and I really think he believes himself. The only thing we are both closer to doing is me finding a way to kill him before Morgan tries to do it for me. Who would have thought I'd have an angel defending me like he likes me and kissing me like he hates me?

"My sons will be coming here tomorrow for the celebrations. They care little for politics, or they would be here today," he tells me, likely to fill in the silence and see my reaction.

"And why do you need me here then?" I ask.

"Where you walk, so shall I, my mate," he says.

"I'm not your mate," I snap. "Stop calling me that."

"Saying that does not make it less real; you are promised for me," he tells me, and I shake my head, knowing there is no point reasoning with the insane lunatic I'm stuck in a limo with. I look out the window, seeing the incredibly tall trees of the forest line we are getting close to. The trees are so closely packed together with big green leaves, so much that when we are under them, it suddenly becomes dark. The trees blur as the limo drives down a bumpy road and comes to a stop, jolting me nearly out of my seat. I sit back up as Lucifer only smiles and pushes the car door open, climbing out far more smoothly than I can manage. I hit my head two times, once on the roof and once on the actual door as I get out and straighten up, pausing at the sight of the massive steel gates we have stopped in front of. The steel looks like woven fabric, and on the top of the gates are wolves made out of steel, frozen perfectly in the act of running after each other. Lucifer stands in front of the limo as the gates open ever so slowly, revealing five rows of wolves waiting on the other side. The wolves stand in perfect lines, row after row, and they are still as statues even as the wind blows dirt around on the ground below their feet. The wolves are mostly black or brown, with a few gray wolves dotted around. I can count at least fifty wolves waiting here, and no one says anything. Suddenly three wolves jump out of literally nowhere, stopping in the middle of the open gates. Two of the wolves I don't recognise, but the one on the left, I would know anywhere.

*Javier.*

"I don't speak mutt," Lucifer comments with a tsk of his tongue. The wolves growl loudly and lowly in response, and I don't blame them. I try to keep my eyes off Javier as I look at the two wolves at his side. The one in the middle has a similar brown colour coat like Javier's, though it is a little darker, and the one on the right is all black and so much smaller that it makes me think it's a female. With one last growl, the wolf in the middle runs to the side of the gate, and the sounds of bones clicking and snapping fills the air before there is silence once more. I risk a glance at Javier's wolf as my hand goes to my arm, covering the scratches there automatically.

I still feel embarrassed and disappointed in him. And I still want to see him. What is wrong with me?

"You stink of wolf death. How many souls did you take, Lucifer?" a deep, roughly spoken voice demands as a man walks out in a deep green cloak, his arms crossed.

This must be the alpha...Javier and Sera's father. They have the same curly black hair, the same deeply tanned skin, and some similar facial features. Mostly it's the eyes that are different between Javier and the alpha though. His father has Sera's eyes, the same rich brown, not the gray stormy eyes Javier has.

"Souls that belong to me can be taken by me at any time, Alpha Trnald Luque. Your grandfather agreed to such a deal many years ago," Lucifer replies, and no one talks for a long while, just a never-ending pause as Trnald stares down Lucifer, and Lucifer stares right back. "Shall I introduce you to my mate, Miss Alexandria Cameron?" Lucifer finally speaks, and I wish he flipping didn't. Javier growls lowly, and everyone looks at him as I step forward, knowing I need to get the attention away from Javier really quickly. Even though I know I shouldn't want to help the bastard that tricked me by pretending to have feelings for me and then left me and the wolves to our own fate.

I tell myself I'm doing it for Sera. Sera loves

her brother, and because of that, I can't get Javier in trouble.

"We have not had the pleasure of meeting," Trnald replies, offering me a hand to shake. I walk forward and shake his hand, even though he almost hurts me with how tightly he shakes my hand back.

"It is lovely to meet you, Alpha Trnald. I heard there is a celebration to be held," I say.

"Yes, there is. My only son, and soon to be alpha, is choosing a mate from a fine collection of wolves from all packs," he tells me.

"I do like a party," Lucifer replies. "But first, we must talk. Perhaps someone can show my mate around the pack as she is uninterested in politics."

"I never said that," I say, because I would like to be there. I want to know what shit storm Lucifer is trying to cook up. "I'm not a stupid girl. I want to be in the meeting to hear and voice my opinion."

"We will talk about it in the limo, dear mate," Lucifer replies, his jaw twitching ever so much that I know I've pissed him off. Oh well, the bastard has at least one emotion even if it is anger.

Empathy is clearly not something the devil wins awards in.

"I will send someone to your quarters within the hour. Follow the wolf; he will lead you to your guest quarters," Trnald states, bowing his head respectfully.

"Understood," Lucifer replies, grabbing my wrist as he passes me and pulls me back to the limo. I get in first, and he shuts the door behind me before grabbing me roughly and slamming me onto the floor of the limo, his eyes turning into pits of fire as my demon replies in response, taking over. I lash my claws across his face, and he slaps me back just as hard, cutting my lip before he wraps his hands around my throat and holds me down with his body covering mine.

"If you ever, EVER, embarrass me in company again, mate, I will punish you in ways you could never think of!" he shouts at me. "Do you understand?"

"I am not yours," I bite out, and he tightens his hand, and fear crawls up my throat as I struggle to breathe. My demon pushes in my mind, wanting to attack him, but I know we can't win alone. She knows it too, but she takes over nonetheless, fighting him off to no avail.

"You will find out that you are, soon. Stop fighting what will happen," he tells my demon, who hisses at him, feeling the same disgust that I do. She backs away just a little so we are almost one person as I feel like I can talk again.

"You can force me all you like to be yours, but you will never, ever own me. I am never going to let you have my soul," I tell him, feeling braver than I should. I'm not even surprised as he leans back and punches me hard in the face, blasting pain briefly making me cry out before I thankfully pass out.

# CHAPTER
# TEN

## I'M SURE THE FAIRY TALE SAID TO RUN FROM THE WOLF, NOT KISS HIM

"*Stop it. You must stop it, Alexandria!" Mum shouts at me, her hands gripping my shoulders tightly, tight enough to hurt. Her eyes are frantic, her hair messy, and sweat pours down her cheeks. "Leo! It's happening again!" It's not just her speaking, there is so much screaming in the room as well as bright blue light.*

"*Mum, help, I-I can't—" I beg her as every part of my body starts to hurt, it starts to burn like nothing before. And I can only scream.*

"*I'm so sorry," Mum tells me before she lets me go and quickly walks away. Seconds later, she comes back with a needle in her hand, and she slams it into my neck as I scream.*

. . .

## RUTHLESS AS HELL

The dream leaves me as I sit up quickly, breathlessly gasping for air as I try to calm down, I try to remember the dream, but I just can't. Something about a needle. Something about my mother. I hate when you have dreams you can't remember no matter how much you try.

"Ouch," I groan as pain bursts into the side of my cheek, and I reach my hand up, feeling the half of my face that is swollen. I suddenly remember everything that just happened, or at least it feels like it just happened. Lucifer punching me. Javier being in his wolf form. I look around the room I'm in, which must be a cabin with its wooden walls and floors. There is a fireplace made out of rough-cut stone, with a fire lit inside it, providing heat for the room. I'm lying on a sofa, a yellow blanket covering my legs, and it falls to the floor as I stand up off the sofa. Everything is a little blurry no doubt from the concussion Lucifer gave me.

*We will make him pay for ever touching us*, my demon whispers into my ear. Her burning anger matches my own, but revenge must be a dish served for dessert because right now, we are in the middle of the dinner, still playing a damn game.

And it can't be for nothing. My parents need to survive this. I miss them so god damn much. I miss Nikoli and Claus, even with their weird ways of showing affection.

I miss Javier.

Almost like I've called him, Javier walks into the room through the only door, and it swings shut behind him as I take in his clothes. A thick gray jumper presses against his chest, defining his muscular build, and he has well-fitted jeans and heavy-looking boots on. His hair is messy, like he has run his fingers through it dozens of times, but somehow it still looks soft. His gray eyes find me like there really is no one else in the room, and I don't want there to be.

God, I hate him as much as I like him.

"Why are you here?" I ask, crossing my arms.

"You're mad at me," he muses, his gravelly voice doing all sorts of things to me that it shouldn't. *He left me.*

"No shit, Sherlock," I reply.

"Come with me; I want to show you something," he asks, holding out his hand.

"No. Where is Sera? Is she safe?" I demand.

"Of course she is. She is my sister," he replies, like I'm crazy to be worried at all.

"Then leave. That's all I wanted to know. Tell her I miss her, Javier," I reply.

"No. Do you miss me?" he asks, taking two steps closer to me, and I take one back, moving towards the fire.

"Why would I have?" I ask, lying through my teeth. I'm not admitting anything more to this wolf. He smirks, taking two more steps forward, and I move right back until the heat of the fireplace lets me know I can't move anymore. The wolf has me cornered.

"I told you not to lie to me, my little demon," he warns.

"You lied first," I respond, arching an eyebrow at him. "You played me, and I was a fool. Is that what you want to hear? That, for me, it was real and fucked up, but it was real. It was so, *so* real, and you hurt me."

"That's exactly what I wanted to hear. The truth," he softly replies, taking two more steps until he is right in front of me. My eyes close as he cups my cheek, and I flinch in pain as he softly touches the swelling he finds there.

"Don't play games with me. I have enough to

deal with, Javier," I warn him, my heart pounding loudly in my ears with every breath I take.

"This isn't a game, Lexi. You were right, I lied. I lied, and I was a fucking coward, because I should never have left the academy without you at my side. And the wolves too, because they were my people whether they were bastards or not." I open my eyes in shock, parting my lips, and he doesn't wait before he kisses me. Oh, holy god, he kisses me. His lips are soft against mine as he takes everything I have, mind, body and soul, in one scorching kiss I know I will never forget. I only flinch when he moves away from my lips and kisses my jaw, his hand cupping the nape of my neck. "I want to take you away from him so he can never hurt you again."

"How do you even know I would go with you?"

"Because you give too much away with your eyes. I know how you feel, Lexi. I think it's only you that doesn't know," he tells me.

"You are so pig headed that you couldn't cope with the possibility that I might not like you," I retort.

"You like me," he smirks.

"Nope," I reply.

"Liar," he replies, and I grin, the grin soon fading as I remember where we are.

"I won't leave, not without my parents. I can deal with him for another week. That's all it is," I say.

"Then what? He won't just let you go, Lexi. He thinks you are his, and he needs you for the war he is going to start. He is planning it with my father now, and everyone is in danger. I know he will use you to win the war he is going to start," he tells me. "And I won't let you be used like that."

"Morgan is making a plan. He will fight him if it comes to that," I say. "There won't be a war. Wait, a war between who?"

"The angels, the ones who banned him from ever returning to heaven. Wait, who is Morgan?" he asks.

"My teacher and—" I pause because I really don't know how to tell Javier this.

"The angel I can smell all over you, I presume?" Javier asks with anger burning in his eyes, and I nod once. Nodding is really my only response right now. Somehow, I've gone from a girl who has never kissed anyone to one who has far more guys interested than I thought possible. Hell, my parents did ask me to date more...though I suspect my line up of guys wasn't what they were thinking. "Tell him he will have me to help him take Lucifer down...as long as he doesn't stand in the way of us being together."

"I will fight him too. I am not weak anymore; my demon is bonding with me, and we are strong," I tell him. "And how exactly can we be together, Javier? It's all messed up."

"It will take more than one angel, one wolf and one nearly complete demon to take down the devil," he replies, more to himself and ignoring my worry about us being together. Apparently, that isn't an issue he is concerned about.

"Maybe the sons of the devil himself might help us," I reply.

"Nikoli and Claus? The ones who left you with their father?" he asks in anger.

"You're leaving me with him too. Don't judge them...but maybe Nikoli might help. Claus, I don't think so..." I drift off, looking away.

"He hurt you?" Javier asks.

"Claus did what he is good at, and he ran away when things got tough. I don't know why it hurts that he did," I admit. "But it's not important right now. What are you going to do? You can't seriously go through with this mating thing?"

"I am going to go through with it because it won't work," he tells me. "Not with anyone but you."

"What? I don't understand," I question, and he looks down at my arm before lifting it up and rolling the sleeve up to reveal the marking. Pleasure bursts through me, strong enough to make my legs wobble as Javier runs a hand over the marking, and it glows green. I look up at Javier as he stares at the marking, an expression I can't quite read in his eyes just before he looks directly at me. "My wolf chose you as his, this is proof. You are the only mate he will ever want or accept, so it doesn't matter if I meet a hundred wolves tonight, none of them will be you."

"Do you choose me though? Or is it just your wolf?" I ask, still feeling breathless and weak kneed. I want to push him onto the sofa and rip off his clothes, and my demon only wants the same. I've never felt this...desperate to make sure Javier is mine.

"I will be honest, at first, I was horrified.

Never in history has a wolf marked a demon for their own, let alone an alpha's son. It's unheard of and dangerous for us both. I knew I marked us both for death if anyone knew...so I thought it would be best for us not to see each other. The ball and Lucifer was just a reason for me to try and push you away and give myself time to figure out what to do. Only, every second I've been away from you has been torture. Hurting you with a lie is something I will always be ashamed of. Always. I have no intention of being anything but on your side, Lexi. I promise never to lie to you again, and one more thing," he adds, pausing and letting go of my hand. He sinks to his knees in front of me and looks up. "I am sorry, so deeply sorry for my actions. Will you forgive me?"

Alpha wolves never say sorry.

He told me that the first day we met.

"I already did," I admit, kneeling down and wrapping my arms around his neck, resting my head on his forehead as we both sit in silence.

In the darkness of our past, we have found something neither of us are going to give up.

Something not even the devil himself can take away.

# CHAPTER ELEVEN

KNOCK ONCE FOR HELL, TWO FOR...

Javier's hot breath blows against my ear for a moment as he leans back and tilts his head to the side to look at me. I'm pretty sure he is going to kiss me again when the door opens once more, and we jump away from each other, only to sigh in relief when I see it's Sera. Sera looks between us for a second, a frown on her pretty face, before she runs to me and hugs me as tight as I hug her back.

"I will see you both later. I have to attend the meeting with Lucifer and my father. You have a few hours before he will be back," Javier says, walking to the door, and I look up at him as he opens it, meeting his gaze and knowing we have a lot of unfinished business. "I made you some cookies, Lexi, your favourites. Bye, and be careful." With that warning, he walks out and the door slams shut. I lean back, looking over my best friend.

She looks happy, though tired and possibly needs some more sleep. Her wavy brown hair is braided, and she is wearing jeans with a white blouse. It looks far better than the uniform she had to wear at the academy.

"How are you here?" I ask her, holding her arms because I don't want to let go. She frowns and reaches up, not touching my cheek but hovering her hand over it.

"Who did this to you?" she demands.

"Lucifer, and it's nothing. I'm more interested in how you are here—"

"How is that nothing? Half your face is swollen, Lexi!" she scolds me. Typical Sera, always caring for me, and I honestly love it. I missed her. "I know this place has a medical box. I will be right back." Before I can tell her not to leave, she runs off into one of the other rooms, and I sink down onto the sofa as I wait for her to come back. My cheek does hurt now she mentions it—seems Javier is a good distraction. Sera comes back and sits on the sofa, turning my face gently towards her before looking through a white box in her hands.

"How are you walking around safely?"

"Javier brought me back to the pack and made it clear that if anyone touches me, including our father, he would kill them. It was pretty terrifying, and I'm sure half the pack nearly wet themselves. Since then, I've moved into the pack house in the room next to Javier's, and for the first time in my life, they are treating me as if I am one of them," she admits with blushed cheeks. "My father is even talking to me, like nicely. I suspect he missed me, but he won't actually admit that."

"You're safe then," I say with a sigh of relief. Sera is like the sister I never had, and I honestly don't think I could cope with losing her.

"Well, until everyone knows about that mark on your arm, yep," she says, tutting at me as she unscrews a tin. The moment it opens, an ungodly bad smell comes out it. "You had to fall in love with my brother, didn't you? It had to be complicated to the point of dangerous for us all. I am happy for you, because you and Javier are as stubborn as each other, but this is all levels of scary and unheard of."

"I don't even know what to say," I admit, and she just smiles at me with a long sigh.

"This stuff smells bad, but it works. It will heal your face within the hour," Sera says, dipping her finger into the red goo and carefully rubbing it on my cheek before I can say no. "God knows what's going to happen when Javier tells the pack he is in love with you and marked you as his own."

"He hasn't said he loves me, and why can't we keep us a secret? The moment he tells anyone, Lucifer will find out and try to kill him. We *have* to keep it quiet," I tell her. "Lucifer is dangerous."

"But he has to choose a mate soon. Father won't let him walk out of the ceremony tomorrow without choosing someone," she tells me, making me worried. "Though Javier is good at sweet talking our father, so he might be able to get out of it."

"Know anyone that would like to pretend to be his mate for a while?" I ask her. "I mean, just for a week or so until my parents' trial. After that, we are going to leave, and if Lucifer follows, Morgan, Javier and I will kill him."

"Morgan? As in the sexy teacher you hate?" she asks with a teasing smile.

"Not so much hate anymore..." I mutter.

"Wow," she chuckles, and I grin, feeling my cheek less sore already as she gets up and finds a towel to wipe her hands. "I'm seriously happy for you, but I'm worried. No, that's a lie. I'm downright terrified for you. I don't want you to die, because you are my sister. Not by blood, but by everything else. You treated me like an actual person when you didn't have to, and not only that, you were always there for me. We might be different, but you have never made me feel like that. I knew we were going to be family one day even if you didn't mate with my brother. We have always had this connection, and I never want to see you hurt."

"I'm not going to die," I say, although the warning Gabriel gives me flashes into my head for a brief second. "I'm too stubborn to die, and I feel the same way as you do. No matter what, I am your best friend and sister from another mother."

"I like that saying, it's cute," she says with a big smile. "Come on, why don't I show you around the pack grounds? Sitting in here, talking about possibly dying, isn't going to make us do anything but worry," she suggests, though her eyes still hold the fear in them that she doesn't want me to see. Shame I know her better than she thinks.

"What about the red crap on my face?" I say, and Sera grins as she shakes her head at me.

"All gone. It absorbs into your skin to heal you. Don't worry," she says, walking to the door and opening it, holding the door as I walk to her side. Sera automatically goes to walk in front of me as we step outside onto a long wooden porch, and I catch her elbow.

"My best friend walks at my side, not in front," I gently tell her, and she blushes as she stops and hooks her arm in mine.

"I forget we aren't at the academy anymore," she admits, and I pause, looking at the forest around us. The cabin we are in is in its own clearing, with picket fencing surrounding the area. Our limo is parked at the side of the dark wooden cabin which is all one level with several chimneys on the roof and a wraparound porch. I can hear the distant sounds of people and smell smoke in the air, likely from a bonfire.

"You aren't a slave, and you won't ever be

again," I tightly say, trying to be happy that she is free, but a tiny part of me is jealous. I want the same freedom she has found; I want more than being at DA. "Honestly, you were part of what kept me sane in DA. Now that you're gone, I only have a talking cat and moody guys to send me crazy."

"Wait, talking cat?" she asks, squeezing my arm in shock, and we both pause, staring at each other. "Amethyst talks? Like actually talks to you?"

"Yes, and I swear I'm not crazy. She has talked to me since I got her from a rescue," I tell her, and it feels good to tell someone about Amethyst. I honestly didn't think anyone would believe me for a long time, but coming to DA, I'm learning a talking cat really, really isn't that strange.

"Why didn't you tell me?" she asks, sounding hurt.

"I thought you'd think I was mad," I admit.

"You know, Amethyst always confuses me. She isn't like a familiar, but she is loyal enough to you to know she cares. Then again, she is always leaving your side, whereas familiars usually always want to be with their owner. I've seen familiars before, and she really isn't one. Now you tell me you can hear her talk to you. That is not normal, Lexi," she tells me. "Plus, familiars have powers, ways to protect and fight beside their owner. Amethyst left you alone with a wolf threatening you, rather than protecting you. It's weird."

"Amethyst isn't normal. By the way, she constantly complains about missing your cooking...and I complain with her," I try to change the subject as my throat clogs up with fear.

"Be careful around Amethyst, Lexi. If she isn't your familiar, then she is a magic cat who shouldn't exist," she tells me. "And it makes me wonder why she is following around the supposed Queen of Hell. She may be using you for a bigger picture that we can't see yet."

"Do you have a library around here? Maybe we can look up talking cat books. I would check the library at DA, but after Morgan said a book killed a student, I'm too scared to open any of the books there," I try to joke, trying to change the subject once more.

"Lexi, I'm being serious, don't try to make a joke of this," she warns me, stepping in front of me and placing her hands on my shoulders. "If

Amethyst is dangerous, she lives with you. She could kill you in two seconds flat."

"I know you are trying to protect me, but I can't add another thing to my already full plate right now. Amethyst is just my cat, who I love and is all the family I have left if my parents' trial doesn't go well. I can't think about this right now, Sera," I admit to her, stepping away and shaking my head. Amethyst is just my cat. That's it.

"I will research what I can and figure it out. It's going to be okay," she says, pulling me into her arms. "Now, for the tour I promised. It will be a good distraction, I promise." I give her a shaky nod and hug her once more, feeling like I won't get another chance any time soon.

# CHAPTER
# TWELVE

A DEMON AND A WOLF ARE DRINKING
IN A PUB...

After walking down the only pathway to the cabin I am staying in, we come to a village in the middle of the forest, full of wooden cabins of all different levels, all within a circle of the clearing, where the sun is shining down on the tops of the cabins, making the light wood glow a soft brown. I feel like there are a dozen things to look at, from the red pebble pathways to the water fountain I can see at the end of the pathway in front of us, looking like it is in the middle of the village. Of all the cabins, one stands out right at the other side of the village, mainly because the cabin is painted green. It's much, much bigger than any of the others here, towering over them almost.

"Welcome to the pack. This is the main part of the pack, but to the left are the fields of plants we grow, and to the right is the hunting area, filled with deer and so much more to keep our wolves busy. The alpha's house is the massive green one you can't exactly miss; that's where I'm living, by the way," she explains to me as I look at the streetlights, the flowers in pots outside the houses, and the general atmosphere of the pack. It's peaceful and quiet. You'd never know they were wolf shifters and they gave away their bastard children to the devil.

"Seeing as Lucifer is going to be there, we should go somewhere else," I say, clearing my throat.

"I have the perfect place. I want you to meet someone anyway," she tells me, nodding her head to the left.

"Let's go," I say, patting her hand hooked in my arm. We make it a few steps before a bunch of young kids run into our path, stopping and staring at us.

"Sera, is your friend really a demon?" a little boy of around eight asks, grinning with two teeth missing and two trusting eyes fixed on me and Sera.

"This is Alexandria, and yes, she is a demon, but mostly she is just like us," Sera explains, leaning closer and fluffing the little boy's hair.

"Wow...do you have horns?" he asks me with wide, innocent eyes.

"Yep," I say, almost laughing when they all giggle and whisper between them.

"We have somewhere to be. Run along, kids," Sera suggests, and they do as they are told, running down another pathway and disappearing behind a house. "Sorry, they don't see anyone new in the pack, let alone a demon."

"It's cool," I say, resting my head on her shoulder. "I don't mind kids." I lift my head when we get further into the pack, passing the cabins, and everyone we pass scans me with distrusting eyes and glares at Sera for being near me, I guess. Luckily, DA made me get used to people staring and made me realise that I really don't care much for what strangers think of me. We get to the water fountain I saw in the distance, and it's much bigger than I thought. It has steel-made trees in the middle of the fountain, and metal wolves running all the way around them, with water pouring from their open mouths in a spiral.

"Did the same person who made the water fountain make the gates?" I ask.

"Yes, one of the first alphas was very creative, and he made all the steelwork in the pack. You will see bits of his work everywhere. Ironically, he was killed by a wolf statue in the alpha house when it fell on top of him. That's why it has a dent near the wolf's mane," she tells me as we get to a door, and she opens the handle, letting us inside. The smell of good food fills my senses as the heat of the room blasts against my skin. Whispered voices drift to me as I look around the bar and the dozens of tables in the room with people drinking and talking at them. Every single one of them turns to look at us, but Sera drags me to the bar and to the staircase at the side of it.

"He is indisposed, Sera," the woman comments, clearly not impressed with whoever "he" is.

"When is he not?" Sera grumbles with red cheeks at the bartender, who only laughs and shakes her head of blonde hair. Sera walks up the staircase first, and I follow her up the wooden, creaky staircase to the row of doors in a corridor at the top. Sera knows exactly where she is going as she bangs her fist on the third door in the row and starts shouting, sounding nothing like Sera.

"Eike Matthews! Javier needs help, so get your pants on and open this damn door!"

"I thought you liked it when I left my pants off, Serafin Luque," a teasing male voice replies, and Sera shakes her head as we hear a female voice complaining from the other side of the door.

"Who is Eike?" I quietly ask.

"Javier's best friend and a giant flirt. We need his help though," she tells me. "Well, you do. He is the only person that might be able to help you."

"Why?" I ask.

"We will talk inside, too many ears out here," Sera tells me as the door opens and a beautiful blonde girl about our age storms past us in a wonky dress, messy hair, flushed cheeks, and her shoes in her hands. Only seconds later, the door is tugged further open by a very sexy red-headed wolf, though he hardly notices me as he looks directly at Sera and pushes a large hand through his thick, curly, dark red locks of hair. He has brown eyes that are similar to the colour of

Sera's hair, and he doesn't have a shirt on, so I can't help but notice his six pack, muscular arms and defined chest. He crosses his arms and leans on the door, biting down on his bottom lip as he and Sera stare each other down.

I really, *really* want to leave them to whatever this is.

"Looking good, little Serafin," he comments with a low whistle, "though I'm surprised to see you knocking on my door."

"I'm not little, Eike. Can we come in?" she sharply asks.

"I've never had a demon in my room before, or you for that matter, Serafin," he comments. "My lucky day, it seems."

"You're a sleaze, that's why, Eike," Sera snaps. "And unless you want your best mate ripping you into tiny pieces, I wouldn't flirt with this demon."

"But *you* want me. It's no secret, Sera," he quickly has a comeback for her.

"In your own head, I'm sure you think that. Let me know when you realise there is a whole world outside of it," she suggests.

"I really missed you, Serafin. I don't know anyone else who calls me out on my shit like you do. Now, this must be Alexandria Cameron," Eike says, turning towards me as the door shuts behind him and offering me his hand to shake.

"You know who I am?" I ask, looking around the small bedroom, littered with clothes and smelling like...well, boy and wolf.

"I'm Javier's best mate; of course I know who you are. He doesn't shut up about you. The boy is obsessed," he tells me.

"Isn't his best friend meant to keep things like that a secret?" I ask.

"Do you not know he fancies you? I thought he had more game than that," he remarks, crossing his arms. Sera just sighs.

"Why do we need his help, Sera?" I ask, feeling frustrated with this guy. He doesn't seem bothered about anything as he jumps on the bed and stretches out, leaning on his side as he grins at us. Sera pulls out two chairs from the table pressed against the wall by the door, and I sit on one as she sits on the other.

"Did Javier tell you Lexi is marked by his wolf? And that he wants her as his mate?" Sera asks, and my cheeks feel like they burn for the first time since we came into this room. Eike looks serious as he sits up.

"Fuck," Eike shouts. "What was the motherfucker thinking?"

"Language," Sera warns.

"Oh shit, I forgot you hate curse words, and I forgot how much I like fucking using them," Eike replies, and Sera looks like she is one word short of stabbing him. "He can't have a demon as a mate. He is going to be alpha."

"I thought there is one way he could be with Lexi, and the pack wouldn't suffer," Sera quietly says. "It would be right…it was always meant to be this way."

"No. Get out, Serafin. You cannot ask that of me. I would do anything for you and your brother. You both know it, but you can't ever ask that of me," he all but growls. Sera doesn't back down as she stares at him.

"Eike, it's your blood right—"

"I said out. My family is all gone because of the blood in my veins and the risk of what I could do. I will not die for you and your brother, Sera," he tells her.

"Then you're a coward just like I've always known you are!" she shouts at him, getting up and walking to the door, going out without waiting a second more.

"She didn't mean that," I gently say.

"She did. Now get out, demon. I have to drink until I forget she ever asked me anything," he growls at me, picking up a bottle of whiskey and downing it like I have already left. I'm so confused about what just happened, but I'm not staying in this room with a stranger. I leave his room, shutting the door behind me and heading to the stairs and walking down. I find Sera at the bar, and to my surprise, she has two glasses of purple liquid in them. It doesn't look like wine, but I follow Sera to a table in the back, ignoring the silence and stares that follow.

"Have you all never seen a bastard wolf and a demon drinking in a bar together before? Get over it!" I raise my eyebrows at Sera's outburst and how she just swore, as I've never seen her this way before. Eike really knows how to wind her up.

"What happened to my quiet friend?" I ask, half joking. "And what is this stuff?"

"It's called Moonshine. It's a famous drink and super sweet," she tells me and takes a long sip at the same time I do. She is right, it's sweet and almost soft to drink. "I'm sorry, Eike has always made a side of me come out that I never liked."

"I kinda like this side to you. You are brave, girl," I say, and she chuckles, the smile soon replaced with a sad smile.

"What happened up there? I don't understand," I admit. "What is his blood right?"

"Eike's family used to be the reigning alphas many, many years ago. When Lucifer came to make a deal with the pack, his great-grandfather said no, and he was killed. Lucifer gave the alpha title to another, my great-grandfather, who was simply a teenager with a strong wolf. Over the years, Eike's family have challenged my family for the alpha title back, and all of them have died for it because Lucifer blessed my family with extra power. Even his mother and sister were killed because they tried to stop my father killing theirs. Javier pinned Eike down on the ground to stop him and saved his life. That was ten years ago," she explains. "But now my father is weak, and Javier...well, you know what he wants. Eike has a chance."

"So you think Eike should challenge—" I whisper, and Sera looks around us, likely making sure no one is listening in before she whispers back.

"My father, yes. Then Javier would be free to mate with whomever, and I know Eike is a good choice for alpha. Javier is as well, but his heart has chosen a path that the pack cannot support," she explains.

"Eike said no," I remind her.

"I know, and I suspected he would. For a few years now, Eike has drunk himself silly and slept his way through the pack to forget the past. A few words from me aren't going to make him change his mind," she muses. "I have to hope he will grow up and be the wolf his family and everyone needs him to be."

"You have feelings for him," I point out.

"No," she sputters out. "Why would you think that?"

"The sexual tension between you two, for one. Wait, did Santino ever escape DA? I imagined he did, but I haven't checked," I ask.

"He did, and in the escape, he met another girl who is actually his true mate. I'm happy for him, because me and him, we hadn't even kissed. He was more a friend," she admits to me.

"There wasn't a spark," I muse. "Not like the spark I saw between you and Eike."

"You must be seeing things, Lexi," she replies, though her red cheeks say more. "Besides, he wouldn't look twice at me. He can have any wolf, and I'm just a half breed with—"

"No, Sera, anyone would be lucky to have you in their lives," I firmly tell her.

"We should finish our drinks and head back," she changes the subject, her cheeks bright red.

"I don't want to go back to that asshole. I wish he just stayed in hell," I admit, possibly a little too loudly as the room goes silent.

"Don't we all, Lex," Nikoli's voice drifts to me, and I look up to see him leaning against the wall next to our table, his eyes fixed on me. He has the school shirt on, sleeves rolled up, the white fabric pressed tightly across his chest. The shirt is tucked into his black trousers, and his shiny shoes reflect the dim lights in here. Nikoli Lucifer is more handsome than should be allowed.

If this is the beauty hell can create, then the world is screwed. His unusually calm purple and green eyes never leave my face, and I never look away from him. "Sera, I will take Lex back to the room. Thank you for showing her around, and it is good to see you well."

"Of course," Sera mutters, pushing her chair out, and the sound snaps me out of the trance Nikoli put me in. I stand up and hug Sera tightly, whispering a warning to her before we leave.

"Don't come and see me again. I don't want Lucifer knowing you mean something to me. He has made it clear hurting me is something he likes to do, and I can't lose you. Stay safe," I warn her.

"And you," Sera tells me, and it feels like I'm losing her all over again. I reluctantly let her go and watch her leave the bar before facing Nikoli.

"I'm sorry my demon threw you out of the window," I say, as I haven't seen him since then.

"Don't be. My demon likes to play rough too and rather liked it," he honestly replies, and I find myself grinning back at him. "Come on, let's go somewhere quiet." Nikoli links his hand with mine, our fingers entwining as we leave the bar. The devil might be here, but his son is welcome anytime.

# CHAPTER
# THIRTEEN

NEVER MAKE A DEAL WITH THE DEVIL.
YOU WILL REGRET IT

"Thanks," I say, accepting the cup of tea from Nikoli, and he sits next to me with his own, sipping quietly.

"Is Claus here?" I gently ask, half hoping he is and half hoping he isn't, because he might ignore me once again, and that hurts more than I care to admit.

"No, he is being an idiot still," Nikoli sourly replies. "Though our father always has a strange effect on him. I'm not making excuses for his behaviour, but it's hard for Claus to be around Lucifer."

"What do you mean?" I ask before taking another sip and eating one of the cookies that Javier made for me. Nikoli has already eaten five of them, and I can't blame him; they are amazing.

"Can you imagine what it's like having the devil as a dad?" Nikoli asks. "Especially for someone like Claus, someone who is playful and really isn't as fucked-up as Lucifer would like him to be. Our human foster mother used to say Claus is too gentle for the world, and she was right. Lucifer can push Claus all he wants, but Claus will just run further away and be who he always has been."

"Considering the time I've known Lucifer, I can't say he is a great influence," I say. "I understand why Claus would run."

"He likes to beat Claus up until he passes out; he loves to break his bones so he can't run away for a little bit. I try to stop him, and he always kills someone I like for interfering. Dad says it will make Claus strong, but I think it only fucks him up to the point he doesn't know who to trust. So yeah, Claus is pissed that the man he hates more than anyone in the world has taken the only girl he has ever wanted," he explains to me.

"Lucifer hasn't taken me," I remind him. "He can't."

"I know he can't. You love us," he says, and I pause with wide eyes.

"Whoa, I've never said that," I whisper.

"You will though. You are ours; I don't care what daddy dearest states. You are mine," he tells me, reaching his hand forward and stroking my cheek with his fingertips.

"I don't belong to anyone, Nikoli. That hasn't changed," I say, though it feels like those are my dad's words and not mine.

"You tell yourself that, Lex," he murmurs, taking my half empty cup of tea out of my hand and placing them both down on the wooden counter. "Tell me you aren't mine when you look at me like you do right now."

"Nikoli, it's too dangerous to think about us. I just want to focus on us all surviving and my parents being free," I admit.

"We are born into dangerous lives, Lex. If we wait for our lives to be normal, we will never get what we want," he tells me, coming back to stand in front of me, his legs pressing into my knees.

"And what do you want, Nikoli?" I breathlessly say. I know what I want, but I don't dare say it out loud.

"You. I want you as fucking mine, Lex. I've always wanted that," he tells me and leans in just as the door slams open, and we jump apart. I couldn't be more disappointed as Lucifer shuts the door behind him, a self-satisfied smile on his stupid face.

"Honey, I'm home!" he happily says.

"Great, now leave," I sarcastically reply, and he frowns. I know I'm being stupid, testing him, and I remind myself I need to play nice.

He holds the power to free my parents or sentence them to death.

"Good idea. Son, get out and find a suit. We have a celebration to attend tonight," he tells Nikoli, who doesn't seem on board with the idea as his eyes flicker between Lucifer and me.

"No—" Nikoli starts to say.

"Nick, it's fine," I stop him. "Go," I gently say, and I see the anger burning in his gaze as he wordlessly gets up and walks past his dad before going out of the front door, slamming it hard behind him.

"Seems my son is still enamoured with you. It's best you stay away from him," Lucifer says as he walks to my side and sits down. I move away from him, pressing myself into the sofa arm as hard as I can. He only laughs. "I have a surprise for you."

"I don't want anything from you, Lucifer," I snap.

"Call me Luc. I have told you many times, are you stupid?" he asks.

"Nicknames are for people who like one another. I don't have any affection for you, so why would I call you a nickname?" I ask, and his jaw twitches in anger as he reaches to grab me, and my heart pounds in my chest as I fear what he is going to do to me. Just then, the door is knocked two times and Lucifer pauses, gritting his teeth loud enough for me to hear as he stands up.

"Come in!" he demands, and the door opens. I look back to see two women with curly brown hair, a little older than me, push in a clothing trolley with a dozen dresses hanging inside. "Good, get out." The women don't pause as they run out of the cabin, shutting the door.

"Try the dresses on. I want to choose which one," Lucifer commands. "We have a celebration to attend tonight, remember?"

"I'm positively shaking with excitement," I mutter as I walk around the sofa and look at the dresses. Three of them are red, but they only remind me of the dress I wore at the ball and the hundreds of wolves that lost their lives that night. It seems disrespectful to wear a red dress so soon, so I look at the two black dresses. One of them has no sleeves, so that's out, even though it is beautiful. The other is made of black lace covering all my arms and falls to the ground. I pick the hanger with that dress off the rail and look back to Lucifer.

"I'm going to try this one on. I will be right back," I say.

"No, try it on here," he says, stopping me in my tracks. Fear and disgust crawl up my throat as I look back at Lucifer.

"Hell no!" I shout at him.

"Do you know how patient I am with you, Alexandria? I am your mate, and soon I will be enjoying your body under me as you will enjoy me inside you," he tells me, and I nearly choke on the sickness that rises in my throat at the thought. I'd rather repeatedly stab myself.

"No," I tell him.

"Fine, I have a deal," he playfully says, clearly choosing to ignore my obvious disgust.

"I've heard the saying *never make a deal with the devil* before," I sarcastically say.

"If you want to dress alone, then I want a token of affection. One kiss," he suggests.

"Is there a third option?" I ask.

"No, and the offer is not going to last long. I have forcefully taken what I want before, and you are testing my good nature. Continue to test me, and I will drag you by your hair into hell and make you mine as you scream for me to stop. After you are mine, I will kill your parents in front of you and then find anyone you care about and kill them too. I will enjoy drinking their blood as you beg me, plead for me, to kill you," he tells me.

"Seems you have it all planned out," I whisper in pure fear. I don't doubt him for a second as I look into his dead-of-emotion eyes. My hands shake as I grip the dress, and I swallow the disgust in my throat. "I will kiss you instead of undressing in front of you."

"Modest, I do surprisingly like it," he says, his personality snapping from psychotic to nice in a second. I'm sure they have a pill for that somewhere. Maybe I can find some and mix it in his drink. "I will accept your offer of a kiss. Now go and get dressed."

"But—"

"Go," he demands, and I don't have to be told twice. My hands shake as I walk down the corridor and open the first door, finding a bathroom. I shut the door and lock it, like locking a door is going to help me escape the devil.

*It won't.*

# CHAPTER
# FOURTEEN

### KISS ME LIKE NOTHING ELSE IN THE WORLD MATTERS

"Do you think wolves like to live in wooden houses because they like trees? My home is surrounded by fire, which I do love. It's strange that the pack have not invested in more materials than wood," Lucifer comments, and his constant talking is getting on my nerves. Does he ever shut up?

"I don't know," I mutter, repeating myself for the fourth time. Who knew the devil likes to talk, like never-ending talking about random shit I don't care about? I feel more and more uncomfortable the further we walk through the silent village, right towards the pack house. I feel Nikoli's eyes burning into my back from behind us, though he doesn't say a word to try and get his dad to shut up. I just feel nervous and am constantly biting my tongue so I don't embarrass Lucifer and get beaten up, but it is starting to hurt my mouth.

"What do you know of wolf traditions, Alexandria?" he asks me.

"Not all that much," I answer, slightly lying. I don't want to explain to him how I know so much about wolves if I gave him a real answer.

"I find it fascinating that wolves can scent their true mate. They will make food for her, showing they can provide, and when the wolf scents they feel the same way, they will mark the female's skin with a wolf marking. The marking is far more than a scratch, it is a bond between the two mates, and when they have sex, it makes an everlasting bond that is unbreakable. If one dies, so will the other," he explains.

"Interesting," I say with a dry mouth, and I gulp, knowing that is exactly what Javier did with me, and I missed it. I'm his mate...and for some reason, it makes me want to smile. That stubborn wolf has stolen my heart without me even realising.

I should be mad.

I'm not though.

"Do you know about demons and our mating traditions?" Lucifer asks as we get close to the building.

"Yes," I tightly answer him, feeling his eyes on me, and it makes me feel like there are dozens of bugs crawling over my skin. "It's all about sex, huh?" I regret it the moment I speak. I don't want to talk about sex with the devil.

"For a virgin, that must be difficult to comprehend. I will help you understand soon," he tells me, and I nearly cough on the rising sickness in my throat at that image. I somehow don't think so. I'd rather jump off the nearest cliff, which can't be too far away on this island. "Once we mate, it will mean one of us cannot die without the other also dying. It is a very interesting magical connection."

"Welcome to the ceremony of choosing," a woman in a silky red dress says as we get to the double doors of the alpha's home. "These are for you. Everyone must wear a mask." The woman hands us each a black eye mask with feathers going off the edges, and lace covering it. Lifting my long hair, I slide the eye mask on, and the woman clicks her fingers, and the doors open, letting us inside the corridor that has a black carpet liner leading to another pair of doors with servants in all black, wearing the same masks as we are, holding silver trays with drinks on them. Between each servant is a statue of a wolf, each in a different pose, each looking more imposing than the next. I wonder which one squished the alpha Sera told me about. The doors at the end of the corridor lead into a big room full of small tables with candles on them. There is a long table at the front, and the whole design reminds me of a wedding reception. To the left is another room with big doors left open so I can see people dancing inside and hear the music that is coming from there.

Every table is filled with women all around my age, all in different coloured gowns, and all are sneaking glances at the long table at the front where I see Javier first. He wears a white mask, different from everyone in the room, and a white suit, which by god, makes the asshole look handsome.

I'm sure he knows it too. I'm sure he also is aware how jealous I am as I realise all these women are ogling him alongside me. At Javier's side is Alpha Trnald, wearing a black suit, and his expression is frosty as he looks at us as we walk past the tables and towards them. At Trnald's side is a woman I haven't seen before, but judging from her hand resting on top of Trnald's, this must be Javier's mother, the alpha female or Omega as I've heard the wolves call her. She is really very beautiful with stormy gray eyes and long jet black hair that is so smooth, not a single hair out of place. She has deeply tanned brown skin, and the black dress she wears is tightly pressed to show her amazing body. She looks not much older than my mum, but there is a big difference.

My mum never looked as downright cold and still as this woman does. I guess I'm a little jaded because I know she killed Sera's mum, who was an innocent, and then made Sera's life hell. I don't like Javier's father for putting Sera's mum in that spot in the first place.

As we approach the table, all three of them stand, and Lucifer grabs my elbow, forcing me to stop next to him. Nikoli walks around to stop at my side, and I sneak a glance at him to find he is looking at me as well.

"Welcome, much honoured guests. May I introduce my son, Javier, sole heir to be the next alpha of the pack," Trnald says, not introducing his mate first, which I thought he would do. Javier doesn't say a word as he stares at us, his whole demeanour shouting how tense and annoyed he is.

I could guess a few reasons why. One being the root of all evil at my side. "This is my mate and alpha female, Mizette."

"It is but an honour to meet you, your highness," Mizette says, sounding as sweet as a child.

"Finally, a woman who knows how to treat her guests. May I have this dance? The ballroom looks ever so delightful," Lucifer says, his eyes fixed on Mizette, who all but giggles as she nods. Maybe she is younger and dumber than I first thought. Good luck to her. I roll my eyes as Nikoli holds a hand out for me to take.

"May I have this dance?" he asks me.

"Actually, as Lucifer has borrowed my mate, it would be suitable for me to steal his. For a dance, of course," Trnald comments, standing up. Lucifer rapidly agrees before I can say a word, and I glance at Javier, wishing he could and would say something to get me out of this. "Javier, please find Nikoli a seat at our table while we are gone."

"Of course, father," Javier tightly replies, and I feel like I'm sweating from the pressure and my own nerves as Lucifer and Mizette walk off to the ballroom through the side door, and Trnald comes to my side, offering me his arm. I hook my arm through his, silence making this all the worse as we head into the ballroom and right into the middle of the dancing people, many of whom smile and bow at Trnald as we pass them. Trnald takes my hand and places a hand high on my back as we dance to the beautiful music played and sung by an orchestra on the other side of the room.

"The singer has a soulful voice," I comment, wanting to say anything to fill in the awkward silence.

"Yes, she is very talented. As are you, I've heard, Miss Cameron," he tells me.

"I wouldn't say that, Alpha Trnald," I reply.

"Your demon is at peace with you before your eighteenth birthday. I have heard that is very uncommon and takes a lot of strength?" he enquires. "I would not expect less from the soon to be Queen of Hell."

"Thank you," I reply.

"I get the suspicion you do not like your mate," he whispers to me.

"He is not my mate, despite what he claims," I tell him.

"But he is destined to be. He can walk where you walk, and only his mate allows that to happen," he comments.

"No offense, but I wasn't brought up in this world. I believe no magic in the world can make you love someone. It is there, or it is not," I reply.

"If you were brought up in this world, Miss Cameron, you would know love has little to do with mating," he warns me.

"Then isn't that a sad world?" I ask.

"Perhaps it is. For a young soul, you seem to be aged beyond your time. I do now see why my daughter speaks so fondly of you. You might judge me for letting her go, but if I could have justified the lives of so many in a war for my daughter, I would have. It's why I let my son sneak out of the pack and go see her. To see you as well, though he has no clue I am aware of such things," he adds, surprising me, and I'm not sure what to say for a long second.

"I believe he underestimates you," I say.

"Oh, my son does. He seems to think I don't

smell his desire for you every time you are near. He thinks I don't know how to see true love in someone's eyes," he comments and laughs. "He thinks I do not know my son."

"Alpha Trnald—"

"Stay away from my son, Miss Cameron. You will only get him killed, and if you love him, then you will want to see him find his true mate tonight," he sternly tells me, still fake smiling as the song ends, and he lets me go, bowing his head low before standing straight. "May the soon to be Queen of Hell live long and true."

"May I cut in?" Nikoli asks, looking between me and Trnald with clear suspicion.

"I was just commenting on how I don't feel very well. Can I leave?" I ask Nikoli.

"Yes, of course. You will tell my father of how Alexandria isn't well and I have taken her back to the cabin?" Nikoli asks.

Trnald inclines his head with a nod, and Nikoli rests his hand on my back as he leads me out of the room and around the side of the tables. I look over once and catch Javier still sat at the table, his eyes narrowing in on me and looking like a wolf that wants to catch his prey. But he doesn't move. He doesn't follow me.

And a part of me is happy he doesn't, it means he is safe.

Another more selfish part of me wishes he followed me and kissed me for the world to see, screw the consequences.

Maybe Alpha Trnald was right. This world cares little for love after all.

## CHAPTER
# FIFTEEN
ONE MORE PUZZLE TO ADD TO THE BOX

"Alexandria, do you want to tell me what the fuck was going on with Alpha Trnald? I was listening to every bit of that conversation, and please tell me you aren't fucking the alpha's son?" Nikoli almost cruelly asks me, his voice dripping anger and jealousy. I don't even blame him. If Nikoli was with another girl, I don't know what I would do. I could hardly cope with Maggie talking to Claus, and touching his shoulder made me lose control.

"I'm not fucking him," I answer, not lying exactly as I walk through the cabin and into my bedroom, switching on the bedside lamp.

"Then it's worse. You love him?" Nikoli asks, and I pause in the middle of the bedroom and cross my arms as I turn around, the bedroom door slamming shut. Nikoli's arms are crossed against his suit, his emotions are threatening to swallow me whole with how he looks at me.

"What if I do?" I ask. "What if I'm wolf marked by him and I love him?"

"I don't care," he tells me, walking to me and placing his hands on my arms. "I don't care if you are marked for the whole fucking world, and I don't care if you need me to accept that you love him. I care if you love me as much as I fucking love you."

"You love me?" I whisper, not expecting that answer from him at all.

"Is it that shocking?" he asks, sliding his hands up my neck. "I think I loved you from the moment you called me on my shit in the gym and weren't scared one bit when I reacted badly. I loved you a little more when I watched you have actual sympathy and mourning for a girl who tried to kill you, when we killed her. Everything from how shit you are at making voodoo dolls to the fact I think you have an imaginary cat as I've never seen her, just makes me love you more. It's us, Lex. It's always been us, and we both know it."

"It's always been us, and yes, I've known it. Even when I was scared you might kill me first," I admit with a small chuckle.

"Sexual tension can be perceived in strange ways," he says for a messed-up excuse.

"I'm not sure—" I start to talk, but he laughs, distracting me. I love to hear him laugh.

"Stop talking," he suggests.

"Oh, okay," I mutter, sinking into his arms as he pulls me tightly against him, kissing me hard and fast, never leaving me a second to think about anything other than Nikoli.

And it's just what I wanted. What I didn't know I needed. Kissing Nikoli makes me forget the world is a cruel place; it makes me forget everything. His lips leave my mouth, and he kisses down my jaw as he picks me up and carries me to the bed, laying me down, all while kissing my neck softly and teasingly.

"Do you like this dress?" he asks me in between kissing my neck.

"Your dad got me it, so what do you think?" I ask, and he nips my neck, making me gasp. He leans back, and I watch as his demon slowly appears.

"You really are beautiful, Nikoli," I whisper.

"Show me your beauty, Lex," he tells me. I close my eyes, feeling my body change ever so slightly so that when I open my eyes, I know I look like my demon now, even if she is leaving me in charge. "You are mine."

"I know," I whisper as he leans down and kisses me. His claws and mine make quick work of ripping our clothes to pieces, letting them fall onto the floor and the bed as Nikoli rolls me on top of him. Nikoli somehow makes his hands shift back, I imagine not to hurt me as he runs his hands up my back and to my neck, where he pulls me back down to his lips, kissing me and exploring my mouth with his tongue. He rolls me onto my back as his hand slides to my breast and to my nipple. I've never been touched like this, and I've never felt pleasure like Nikoli somehow manages to give me. His thumb rolls my nipple around, pinching and squeezing as he watches my every reaction before flattening his hand and sliding it down to my stomach.

"I want to touch you as you touch me," I say against his lips, pushing him onto his back.

"Not this time. I will finish in your hand if you do that," he explains to me, and I grin for a second, only to gasp as he slides a finger inside me at the same time his thumb rubs my clit in smooth, perfect rhythms. I forget the world as pleasure blasts through me, making my body shake, and I blink in a haze as Nikoli settles himself over me, and I widen my legs. I look down to see his cock is long and hard as a rock as he gently presses the tip into me.

"I've never—"

"I know. It might hurt a bit, but we will take it slow," he tells me, kissing me softly. "Just don't close your eyes. I want to look into your beautiful eyes as I slide inside you for the first time."

"Nikoli," I whisper, never breaking eye contact as he slides inside me, and oh fuck, it hurts when he breaks past the barrier he finds there.

"I promise to always protect you and love you, Lexi," he groans against my lips.

"I love you," I whisper, feeling a tear escape my eye and roll down my cheek. He kisses me harshly as the pain disappears into pleasure, the pure pleasure of having him fill me. He thrusts out, only to sink right back inside me. He reaches between us as he kisses me, as he thrusts into me, and his thumb rubs my clit, making the pleasure so, so much more. I whimper and moan, my nails digging into Nikoli's back as I come once again, this time stronger than the first, and it is followed by Nikoli groaning.

"Fuck, Lexi," he moans into my ear as he finishes inside me, and he kisses me softly. Suddenly something is wrong as it feels like someone is cutting my arm. I cry out at the same time Nikoli groans in pain, pulling out of me and sitting up, holding his wrist out. The pain is soon gone, and I sit up, looking at my arm in the light. Near my wrist, on my arm that doesn't have the wolf mark, is a silver drawn horse. I run my finger over it, feeling that it stings, just as Nikoli holds his arm out next to mine. In the same place on his wrist is a galloping horse in silver.

"What is this?" I ask Nikoli.

"I don't know. I thought it might be us bonding as mates, but I've never heard of a horse tattoo appearing. Usually you feel a bond, nothing more. I feel the bond, do you?" he asks me, cupping my cheek. The horse mark makes me think back to what Gabriel said to me. If anything, that freaks me out more.

"Yes," I honestly say.

"That means my dad is a liar. You are my

mate, so what does he want from you?" he ponders.

"I don't know. Honestly it makes everything creepier," I admit.

"We will be careful. You must hide the mark, and I will find out what it means," he says, pulling me into his arms and wrapping us in the blanket.

"The world might be dangerous for us, but I will never regret this night. I love you," I tell him.

"Lex, nothing in any world could make me regret having you as my mate," he tells me, rolling me onto my back and pressing himself into me, making me arch my back in pleasure. "I love you, and we aren't done tonight."

"Good. I want more," I say, and he grins, leaning down and kissing me. In the darkness of the world, we have found a little bit of light.

# CHAPTER
# SIXTEEN

WHO WOULD WIN IN A FIGHT? WOLF
OR DEMON?

JAVIER

"You know it's creepy to climb through someone's window in the middle of the night?" I ask as Nikoli Lucifer closes my bedroom window shut. The room is dark, fitting for a demon and perfect for a wolf. I see better in the dark than I do in the light. Rain pours harshly outside, and it drips off the demon's coat onto my wood floor, every drop making the situation more tense. I growl as I lean forward on my chair in the corner of my room, watching the demon closely. Even though he is soaking wet, I can still smell Lexi's scent on him.

It makes my wolf angry.

It makes me want to kill him. He has taken her as his mate. Luckily, Lucifer won't be able to tell; he can't scent them like I can.

"Alexandria would claim I'm good at being creepy," he remarks rather proudly.

"What the fuck do you want, demon?" I growl.

"You are going to get Lexi killed. Your father knows everything from your little habit of sneaking into her room at DA to see your sister to the fact you are in love with her," he tells me, and I'm shocked into silence for a moment. I didn't expect that.

"He doesn't know everything," I say, because it's true. If he knew she was marked to be my mate, he would have tried to kill her.

And I would have never let him do that.

"Luckily. I know finding out you wolf marked her and see her as your mate would cause a few issues between you and your dad," he states. Clearly he knows everything. I already hate the smug demon.

"She is mine," I growl lowly.

"And mine," he replies, and there is a tense,

pressure-filled silence as we glare at each other. I move first, jumping off the chair and landing on him, knocking him to the ground as my fist finds his cheek. I lift my other fist as he slams a good firm punch into my stomach, knocking the air out of my lungs. I growl as he shoves me off him, knocking me across the room so I slam into the frame of my bed. I move quickly, crouching down and growling as the demon wipes blood off his lip and really lets the game start to play as his demon comes out. Large black horns stretch out his head, curling up in the air, and his eyes flash green, a burning green. He points a long, black covered, sharp nailed finger at me and curls it. Growling, I jump in one smooth motion and slam into the demon, both of us smacking into the wall hard enough to crack it. Nikoli curls a sharp nailed hand around my neck as I shift only my hands into paws and claw at his chest, my wolf enjoying the scent of his blood.

"Stop that right now!" Sera demands, and I didn't even hear her come in. We both pause, covered in blood and burning with anger as my sister flicks on the light and shuts the door behind her. "This will hurt Lexi if she ever found out. How can you both be such idiots?"

"This is because—"

"I don't want to hear it from either of you. Lexi needs you both to grow up and get over the fact she loves you both. Don't you get it? Lexi is suffering, she is scared for her parents, she is scared of the new world she doesn't know and all the dangers that come with loving you both. Everything is terrifying to her, and I admire the fact she still gets out of bed every day and tells the devil no, even though it would be easier to just give in. Lexi needs a wall of protection so she doesn't crumble, and by god, you two are part of that wall. Don't you dare let her down because of jealousy," she all but shouts at us.

"You're making me feel shit, wolf," Nikoli grumbles, wiping his lip of blood as I cross my arms. He is right, Sera has us there.

"Well, you are both acting as such all on your own. Nikoli, you shouldn't be here. No one is protecting Lexi from your father while you are here fighting," she says.

"He is busy fucking my mother, so that's not a problem," I add in.

"Gross," Sera frowns.

"Doesn't your dad get jealous and mad?"

Nikoli asks. "Because otherwise that is some fucked-up shit."

"My father only loved one woman, and it was never my mother," I say, looking at Sera, whose eyes speak things we don't talk about.

He loved her mother. Her innocent and sweet mother. I wish every single day that I had been older and could have stopped my mother from killing Sera's mum.

"My father loves no one but himself, so maybe they are a good match," Nikoli replies.

"I don't like this situation, but Sera is right. Lexi needs us to be her wall to make sure she doesn't fall," I say, rubbing the back of my neck.

"It's going to be complicated. Maybe we should have a drink and get to know each other," he suggests. I walk to my desk and open the drawer, pulling out a bottle of Jack Daniels and undoing the lid before taking a long sip. I offer the bottle to Nikoli who tilts his head to the side and nods in respect as he takes the bottle from me.

"I'm going back to sleep. Night, guys," Sera says, leaving the room.

"Jack Daniels is my favourite drink. Maybe you aren't so bad, wolf," Nikoli comments.

"Share then, demon." I hold my hand out, and he laughs, passing me back the bottle. *Share* is the magic word in this situation.

And I've never been good at sharing.

*How can one little demon with big, bright cerulean blue eyes make me change my mind about everything?*

# CHAPTER
# SEVENTEEN
### THE PRICE OF LIES

"Turns out we have to leave for a bit, my love," Lucifer comments as I chew on a piece of toast. "Shame, I was just beginning to like the pack, but business at the academy calls. I do have war to plan."

"A war?" I innocently ask, even though Javier has told me about his plan to make a war with the angels. I need to tell Morgan, and maybe Morgan can warn Gabriel and the others. I'm sure it won't get that far...but if anyone knows a way to make the angels safe, it's going to be Gabriel.

"With the angels," he answers, watching me far too closely as I put my toast down, losing my appetite altogether. "Are you ready to leave? I sense you like the pack life."

"I'm ready to leave," I half answer his question, choosing not to comment on how, yes, I like pack life. Just then, Nikoli walks into the kitchen, not saying a word as he goes to the fridge and gets a bottle of orange juice out before facing us.

"We are leaving today, son," he says.

"Good. This place stinks of wet dog," Nikoli comments, and Lucifer laughs, though Nikoli winks at me behind his father's back.

"It will give you a few more days to enjoy the academy before your parents' trial," he suggests, and I simply nod, trying not look at Nikoli too much and give away that Nikoli is the only person in the room I am interested in talking to. The next hour, we pack our bags, and two Hellers place them in the limo before driving us to the gates of the pack, where the limo stops. I get out after Lucifer, with Nikoli following after me, his hand briefly brushing against mine as he stops at my side, looking at Alpha Trnald, the alpha female, Mizette, and finally, Javier as they walk to us.

"I look forward to seeing you again soon," Trnald comments, bowing his head at Lucifer.

Mizette smiles so widely I wonder if it hurts her face, before she bows, not saying another word. Javier steps forward, locking eyes with Lucifer, and my heart pounds in my chest as I watch them both. *Don't do anything, Javier.* I mentally beg him to back down, but I know he won't.

"It's such a shame you haven't found a mate yet, Javier," Lucifer comments, almost teasingly.

Trnald intervenes, "It sometimes happens. I have found out that not all female wolves came to the celebration due to travel issues, with how the world is suffering at the moment. There will be three more celebrations over the next few weeks, and I am certain Javier will find his mate at one of them."

"Wouldn't that be a delight?" Lucifer comments, and I look down at the ground, gritting my teeth as my demon anger makes my hands turn black and my sharp nails dig into my thigh. The pain keeps me under control, oddly enough.

"My mate will see me soon, I am positive of it." I look up, finding Javier's eyes on me as I understand his carefully decided words. My demon retreats, letting me have control back, and I tuck a piece of my hair behind my ear as I relax. Lucifer says some more pleasantries before we get back in the limo, and I look out the back window as we drive away from the pack.

It feels like I'm driving away from a piece of my heart I can't take with me. I doubt I ever will be able to.

"Why did Claus not come to the pack? Is he not interested in his father's business?" Lucifer asks Nikoli.

"Claus hates travelling; that is all it is, father," Nikoli replies.

"We will discuss when we are home. It is a sign of disrespect that one of my sons didn't come here when I demanded his presence. Living with humans has made you both soft and under the belief you can do as you wish when you cannot," Lucifer angrily comments, resting his hands on his knees. I meet Nikoli's eyes and see the slight glimpse of fear and loathing, and I remember that Nikoli said Lucifer likes to hurt Claus.

This will be a reason to hurt him, and it's all my fault. He didn't come here because he is avoiding me after everything.

A silly part of me hates the idea of anyone hurting Claus, even when I'm mad at him. That silly part of me speaks before the rest of my brain can stop it.

"It was my fault, I told him you said he should stay behind. I wanted someone to watch my cat," I lie, and Nikoli knows it. He knows Lela is watching and feeding Am for me.

"Did you now?" Lucifer very calmly muses, and in the blink of an eye, he pulls a dagger out of the inside pocket of his suit jacket and throws it into my arm, pinning me to the leather seat behind me as I scream. I cry as I try to move the dagger, and my vision blurs as Nikoli shouts. Thick blood pours down my arm as my vision comes back, and the pain seems somewhat worse. I see Nikoli is being held back by Lucifer, a dagger pressed against his neck, and his demon is fully in control. His eyes are as green as his fathers, his horns dig into the top of the limo, and his long nails grip his father's arm tightly, trying to move him away.

Lucifer is too strong though.

"I am tired of you teenagers ignoring me and doing as you wish. Now, Alexandria, you are keeping that dagger in your arm for the rest of the trip back to the academy. I'm sure the bumpy roads will be pleasurable for you," he jokes as I grit my teeth from the pain, and tears fall down my cheeks. I try to keep my arm still, but the moving limo doesn't help that. Every jolt hurts so much that I want to scream. "Son, you can watch. Learn what happens when I am disobeyed."

"And if I don't watch?" he challenges.

"D-don't," I tell Nikoli who locks his eyes with me. "J-just look. Please, just look." Nikoli looks furious, but he listens to me, and Lucifer moves the dagger away from his son's neck. I keep my eyes locked on Nikoli's for the entire journey, drawing strength where I can, and he is the only thing that stops me from passing out.

# CHAPTER
# EIGHTEEN
## WELCOME HOME...OR MAYBE NOT

I leave the first aid room with a bandage wrapped around my arm and an angry demon mate at my side. Nikoli is visually shaking with anger as we silently walk through students and back to my room, where we both pause outside.

"You shouldn't have done that for Claus. He didn't fucking deserve it," Nikoli tells me.

"Don't tell him, okay? Promise me, Nick," I ask him.

"He never deserved you for more than one second," he tells me, and I don't reply. I really don't want to talk about Claus with Nick.

"You should go and see him. I'm just going to

rest," I say, and Nick steps closer to me for a second, resting his forehead against mine, and I close my eyes, enjoying having him this close even though it is risky. When I open my eyes, he is walking away, and I watch him go until I can't see him anymore.

"No! Don't you dare do it!" I hear Lela scream from the other side of the door. I use my key card and open the door, walking in to see Lela hovering near the counter and Amethyst sitting on it, her paw slowly pushing Lela's expensive looking phone nearer and nearer the edge. I can practically hear Lela thinking of ways to kill Amethyst, and I can imagine Amethyst is laughing. Just as Amethyst pushes it off, Lela jumps and just catches the phone before it would have smashed onto the floor.

"You should get a case for that," I nervously suggest, catching both their attention.

"Finally, you are home. This demon is a moron," Amethyst tells me as Lela stands up, pushing her hair from her eyes.

"Your cat is literally the devil! I am never babysitting it again!" Lela frustratedly shouts.

"What did she do?" I carefully ask.

"What didn't she do is the better question. We can start with her jumping out of closets to scare me, and the fact that every single day, she has left a dead rat in my bed. In my own apartment! How the evil thing gets in there, I don't know! I'm out of here." Lela practically runs from the room, slamming the door shut behind her, and I shake my head at Am.

"Why?" I ask, walking into the lounge and sitting down. "Just why?" Amethyst jumps off the centre and onto the sofa before sitting on my lap, purring innocently.

"I don't like her, and I only like you," she tells me like that is an excuse.

"I want to tell you off, but I just don't have the energy right now," I admit. My arm hurts, and the blood loss is no doubt making me tired.

"Because you missed me. I'm the best thing in your life, we both know it," Amethyst claims.

"I wouldn't go that far," I chuckle.

"I would. You know, I watched a YouTube video of a man who has his cat's face tattooed on his back. I think you should do the same. It will make me very happy with you and forget the whole abandoning me with the terrible teenage demon thing I need to get revenge for," she suggests.

"Sometimes, I really, *really* don't know what to say to you," I admit.

"A simple *yes, I will book it right now. Why don't we set the camera up and take a hundred photos of my face so we can choose the best one*, is what you should say," she tells me.

"Amethyst, you're crazy, but I love your crazy," I laugh.

"I'm not crazy, I'm a cat. That isn't possible. Anything I do is cute, not crazy. Get the right *C* word, Alexandria," she mumbles.

"I know another *C* word that I'm sure Lela is calling you right now," I admit.

"I'm sure the dead snake in her bed will make her love me all over again," Amethyst replies with humour in her voice.

"Oh Am," I mutter.

"Your uncle sent another note. It's on your bed," she says, stretching out before jumping off my lap. I don't know what is creepier, that Amethyst can read or that she thinks dead animals left on beds is a nice present. I walk to my bedroom, kicking off my shoes before I pick up the letter on my pillow. I break the plain red wax seal on the back before pulling out the letter and reading it.

*For my niece,*
*I am happy to report your parents are doing well and are ever hopeful to hold you in their arms soon.*
*As for the situation at The Demon Academy, I wish to speak to you alone on the matter and to advise that caution is always to be used. Do remember the words of my first letter, as they are far more important now than ever before.*
*There is a saying in our family, one your mother and I made up as teenagers in DA.*
*Death is a sweet release from the pain of life. Only in death is your soul truly free.*
*Our souls are worth more than our lives. Remember that, Alexandria. For if the trial does not go as planned... Well, I do not wish to say more.*
*I will always be your family.*
*Your uncle,*
*Harry Snowden*

"My parents are not going to die, uncle," I angrily comment as I rip the letter up and throw it into the bin in my room, just as someone clears their throat.

"Morgan," I smile as I turn to see him leaning against the door frame.

"Miss Cameron, good to see you home from your trip," he tells me, and his gravelly voice is so soothing to hear. Damn, I missed him.

"It's good to be home," I reply, and he straightens up, walking over to me with an angry thin line of his lips. He grips my arm and starts rolling up my sleeve, and I'm thankful it isn't the arm with the wolf mark. I really don't want an argument with Morgan about this right now, though he sees the horse mark. For a moment, he stares at it before muttering something under his breath I can't hear.

"What did he do to you?" he asks me. "Is this horse for Lucifer or someone else?"

"It doesn't matter," I say, pulling my arm back.

"It does. Every single time he hurts you, I'm going to make him fucking suffer for it over and over again," he tells me. "And as for the horse mark, keep it hidden. I suspect it means something, but until I can speak to Gabriel, I cannot confirm my thoughts."

"It's not long until this nightmare is over and we all can leave," I say. "We could find somewhere to hide, to wait out until Lucifer goes back to hell and leaves us all alone."

"Maybe," he says, crossing his arms, and I rest my hands on top of his, just like they are meant to be there. He doesn't move, but he doesn't push me away like I'm almost expecting him to. I still remember his lips against mine, the way he kissed me like there was only us in the room.

The way I wish he would kiss me now.

"We have training tomorrow morning at six and every morning following that. I expect you not to be late," he firmly tells me.

"I'd never be late, Mr. Morganach," I tease, and he chuckles, moving his hand to caress my cheek.

"Do you know how much I want to kiss you? The kiss that your eyes are begging me to do?" he asks me.

"Why don't you then?" I suggest.

"Because if I kiss you again, I won't be able to stop," he warns me. "And you don't understand what that means."

"I'm not telling you to stop," I whisper,

getting lost in his voice, in him being so close to me.

"With you, it's different," he tells me.

"Why?" I ask, locking my eyes with his.

"I—"

"Morgan, fancy seeing you he—" Nikoli freezes mid-sentence, and I frown, wishing he hadn't. Dammit. Morgan steps away from me only to turn around as Nikoli pushes his way into the room and kisses my cheek as he stops at my side.

"Morgan—"

"Tomorrow morning, Miss Cameron. Do not be late," Morgan snaps, and I shake my head as I watch him walk out of my room.

"Sharing you is never going to be easy for him. For any of us," he softly warns me.

"No, it's not. It damn hurts," I mutter as I press myself into his chest.

"Love is a sweet disaster, Alexandria," he tells me.

"Perhaps. Maybe it can be a sweet story instead," I counter. A girl can hope. I got myself into this mess after all.

"We live in The Demon Academy, Lex. Nothing is sweet here," he chuckles and wraps his arms around me, kissing my forehead as he does.

Nikoli is wrong, some things are sweet just like he is with me. My lips tilt up. One of the sons of the devil is sweet as much as he is a monster.

And he is all mine.

CHAPTER
# NINETEEN
BORN IN FIRE? OUCH...

"Sit there," Morgan demands the second I walk into the library, and I frown, looking down at the two cushions on the ground in the middle of a chalk drawing of three circles and a star around them. Trusting Morgan, I sit down and cross my legs, as he moves to sit on the other cushion opposite me. The library has soon become our safe place, and I start to get excited for any moments we can have here, hidden away from the eyes of the academy.

"Good morning, Mr. Morganach," I say.

"Are you ready to learn, Miss Cameron?" he asks me, totally in teacher mode.

"Depends on what you are teaching, Mr.

Morganach," I tease him, because I full well know what we are practising today.

"Holy fire, like we discussed," he replies, and a small smile tilts my lips up, mainly because he is so serious I really don't think he got my suggestive reply. I might possibly need to work on my flirting. I thought I was doing it well, but I don't have anyone to ask for hints. Lela is too much, and any advice she might give me would no doubt scare off any man. Sera is too far away, and considering she is single and shy, I'm not going to be getting any good advice there.

"So what are the chalk lines for?" I ask as Morgan finishes up the inside circle by connecting the gap he left.

"It is holy chalk, and it means that nothing outside of this circle will escape unless I wish it. Now, as I am an angel, holy fire cannot hurt me. You also cannot hurt yourself with holy fire you conjure, it is an impossibility," he explains to me. "So while we are inside this protective circle, we are safe, and so is everyone else if this goes wrong."

"Why doesn't holy fire hurt angels?" I ask him, curious.

"We are born again within holy fire. After our

human deaths," he tells me, a rare detail about angels as he never really speaks about his own kind. I get the feeling Morgan never wanted to be an angel and he never has seen it as a blessing.

"Born in fire? That sounds like it hurts," I gently reply.

"Very much," he bitterly tells me. "The pain doesn't leave your mind for years, and The Angel Academy makes sure you suffer other pain to keep you on your toes."

"Morgan...what is the job of an angel?" I ask. "What is so important that all the pain is worth it?"

"Angels come in pairs, one light and one dark. Dark angels are like devils on your shoulder, able to whisper your deepest and darkest thoughts. Dark angels are alluring, seductive and everything you know you want but shouldn't. Light angels are the opposite, they only whisper things to you that are good and kind, as is their nature. When angels finish The Angel Academy, they are paired with their life partner, and then they are assigned a human who is of importance to the world," he tells me, and I try to take it all in. That is a lot of information, but I know where the devil on your shoulder saying comes from now.

"Of importance?" I ask.

"It could be a baby who will one day be president, or a lonely girl who has had a bad life, so she needs to find her way before doing something very good…or bad. We are never told what the human will be, only that they are our charge. We become their guidance system until their deaths, and then we are reassigned," he explains to me. "Every five humans, we are allowed twenty years off work to find love or a life. Whatever we wish."

"So angels can have children?" I ask.

"Yes, but they don't go to The Angel Academy. Children of angels are free to do as they wish in the angel community, they don't have to pay a price of being brought back to life like we do," he tells me, sounding angry about the whole system.

"Was your best friend your partner?" I softly ask.

"Yes," he tells me and clears his throat, changing the subject like I thought he might do. "Now, to conjure holy fire is much simpler than you would think. Holy fire is within your soul.

You only need to close your eyes, use your demon powers to conjure a fire in your hands, and then open your eyes. You have to believe it is there. It is all in your mind, Miss Cameron."

"Okay," I say, and I close my eyes, holding my hands out together in front of me. I roll my shoulders and call to my demon, feeling my body change in a moment. We are getting quicker at bonding every day, to the point it feels natural to be in my demon form. My demon hardly talks to me anymore; she doesn't have to because I know what she wants.

She is me after all. I imagine a glowing ball of fire in my hands, a green spiralling sphere of holy fire that cannot hurt me. My hands feel hot as I open my eyes, and there in my hands is a sphere of holy fire just like I imagined. Morgan covers my hands and moves them up around our heads.

"Imagine the holy fire spreading around us like a dome," he instructs me, but I don't close my eyes as I do as he requested. The holy fire spreads out like a wave in a dome shape, covering us as it burns around us until it hits the floor. The circle keeps it in a perfect dome as Morgan pulls my hands down and smiles at me as the dome holds itself up.

"I can't believe I did that," I say in amazement.

"You are a natural with holy fire," he tells me, still holding my hands. Before I've thought about it any longer, I move to my knees right in front of Morgan and press my lips to his. I can tell I've surprised him as, for a second, he doesn't move, and then he kisses me back, wrapping his arms around my waist and pulling me against his body. I glide my hands into his hair as I tilt my head to the side and gently bite down on Morgan's lower lip. The gentle bite sends him into a frenzy as he kisses me harsher than ever before, and I love every second of it. I go to undo his top button, wanting this to go further, but he catches my hand and rests his forehead against mine, breathing heavily.

"Not like this. Not in a library when anyone could walk in," he gently tells me, moving my hand away, and I can't help but feel disappointed. The dome of holy fire burns away into nothing but embers as I stand up and rub my shoe on the lines to break the circle before heading to the door. I look back once, seeing my angel on his knees, his head bowed, and my heart thumps so loudly. I get the feeling we will never get a chance to be what we want.

It's too messed up between us.

And it hurts to walk away.

I ALL BUT slump down into my chair in voodoo class, avoiding Maggie who I can feel glaring at me from the other side of the room. The other students flood into the classroom, followed by Mrs. Iversen, who looks extremely peachy for a regular day at DA. Crossing my arms, I notice Mrs. Iversen is looking towards the door as we all wait in silence. I'm thrown a bit when Claus walks in, his gaze cold and empty. In this moment, he reminds me of his father a lot more than I'd ever like to see.

"Claus has a surprise for us all today!" Mrs. Iversen says in excitement. "Well, bring them in." Claus clicks his fingers, and his eyes find mine as five guys walk into the room, in a straight line with glazed green eyes and blood dripping down their bare chests. They are like zombies as they stop in front of the teacher's desk and face us. The guys are all blond, all muscular and remind me of the guys I once saw Claus and Nikoli using in a weird ritual.

"Claus has so kindly offered to let us use his new stock to test our dolls on. I want you all to make a new doll that looks like one of these fine mortals," she says with a lusty sigh. Crazy bitch.

"Claus, have you lost your mind?" I ask, standing up with more confidence than I should have, but this has gone too far. I walk right up to Claus, placing my hands on my hips and staring him down as he stays silent.

Cold.

Empty.

Lost. So very, very flipping lost.

"Please sit down, Miss Cameron, you are making a scene," Mrs. Iversen demands.

"Are you going to make me sit down and risk pissing off Lucifer?" I ask, using the only card I can think of.

"Need my daddy to protect you?" Claus sarcastically asks. *Asshole.*

"No, I'm not the one with clearly fucked-up daddy issues, Claus!" I shout at him, waving a hand at the line of guys who look just like Lucifer. "Whoever these guys are, it isn't their fault. You can't be this evil."

"I never said I was the good guy," he reminds me. Trust me, I never thought for a second he was, but there is a big difference between being the bad guy and being completely evil.

"You never said you were the monster either. Turns out the apple doesn't fall far from the tree," I state.

"In your case, no it didn't. You are as much a betrayer as your parents," he angrily replies, trying to hurt me. Only my parents aren't betrayers, so I don't care.

"Fuck you, Claus. What is wrong with you?" I ask, placing my hands on my hips.

"You would know," he whispers to me. "Seeing as you fucked my brother and forgot about me."

"It's not like that," I whisper back.

"Have we got a problem that isn't personal? I do have a class to carry on with," Mrs. Iversen says, reminding me that everyone is watching us.

"Seems Miss Cameron doesn't like the guys I've chosen. I will have to get some new ones more to her taste," he replies. "Are angels even an option?" *I can't believe he just said that.*

"Oh well," Mrs. Iversen comments, and

before I can say a word, she blasts a wave of holy fire into the guys, and they all scream as they burn right in front of me. I gasp and nearly fall back into the desk as I can't look away.

I do see Claus running away once again as he leaves the classroom.

That's it. Claus Lucifer is going to pay for being an asshole. I won't give up until he does.

# CHAPTER TWENTY

## THE DAY I'VE BEEN WAITING FOR

"I thought Pinocchio was your favourite film. Though I do like Thor, most likely not for the same reasons as you." I nearly jump off my bed when I hear Javier's voice, and I turn to see him in the doorway. I press pause on the laptop in front of me and softly smile at him. He has a dark gray jumper on, with heavy looking boots and black jeans. The gray of the jumper makes him look more tanned, and his own light gray eyes really stand out.

"Tell the wolf to leave. It's late," Amethyst grumbles from her place near my pillow. I set aside my laptop and walk to Javier, who smashes his lips onto mine the second I am close enough.

Seeing as I had the same thought, I kiss him back just as passionately as he lifts me up and carries me into the lounge. He sits down with me on his lap, my legs parted and making me fully aware of how hard he is, even hidden by his jeans.

"How did you get in?" I ask, breaking away from his lips. He moves my hair over my shoulder, and I'm thankful I decided to wear a red tank top and little shorts. I really, really don't want much space between us. He drops his lips to my shoulder, ever so softly kissing me.

"I found an open door. The Hellers are being lazy protecting the academy with Lucifer here; they didn't notice me pass them. They all seem to be arguing about who is taking the meal to Lucifer next so they get to meet him," he explains to me, still pressing kisses to my shoulder blades. "I wanted to see you before tomorrow."

"You know then," I mutter.

"I gather that is why you are awake at four in the morning," he replies.

"What if…" I drift off, not even able to say the words out loud.

"No, don't think like that," he tells me, brushing my hair away from my cheek. "Whatever happens, you won't be alone. I'm here." Instead of answering him, I kiss him and push him over onto his back before climbing on top of him. I pull my red tank top off, watching as his eyes turn into the gray rain cloud of storms that I love to see.

"Are you sure?"

"I've always been sure about you, Javier," I answer before I lean down and kiss him. He groans against my lips as we passionately kiss and rip each other's clothes off, both of us desperate for each other. We have always come together in a battle of love, and this will never be any different.

I never want it any different. Javier reminds me that I'm alive and fighting for everything I have.

I will always fight for him. Javier lifts my arm and kisses my wolf mark, which starts to lightly glow as pleasure bursts throughout my body. His lips travel up my arm and down past my collarbone as his large hands hold my hips down. My back arches as his hot tongue flicks over my nipple, only teasing before he travels further down my body. His large hands hold my thighs apart as his tongue finds my core, and I lose all control. Javier sends me crashing over the edge of an orgasm before he lifts me up and lies on his back, letting me have control.

"My mate," he gently tells me as I line up his cock at my entrance. I slowly sink down onto him, letting him fill me up. "Fuck, you feel too good." I roll my hips as he grips my waist, and I gasp at the intense pleasure, the connection between us as we both chase our ending. Javier suddenly lifts me up and turns me over onto my knees, before parting my legs and thrusting into me, the new position feeling intense and amazing. His teeth graze my shoulder as I get so close to finishing. "You are mine," he growls, and he bites me. The pain is brief as an orgasm blasts into me, so strong that I cry out in pure pleasure as he finishes at the same time. My arm burns once again, like the time with Nikoli, and Javier growls as he pulls out of me and holds his wrist out. I look down at mine as I sit down and see a second horse in front of the other one, and this one is silver too.

"What is this?" Javier asks me, pulling me onto his lap.

"I really have no clue," I admit, and I turn to

Javier. I wrap my arms around his neck as he smiles down at me and kisses me softly.

"Are you tired?" he gently asks.

"No, you?" I ask.

"Not even one bit," he replies, and I squeal as he picks me up and carries me off the sofa.

"Where are you taking me?"

"To shower you. I want to wash you down before making you dirty all over again," he tells me and kisses me before I can reply. I wasn't going to complain anyway.

"You should stay in my room and leave after me," I suggest to Javier as I finish pulling my hair up into a ponytail.

"I will keep him company," Amethyst says, rubbing herself against his leg. He obviously can't hear her, but he frowns at Amethyst anyway.

"I will stay until after the trial. Sera and Eike are covering for me," he tells me. "I want to be here for you; that is more important than my father noticing me missing."

"I would like that," I admit, wrapping my arms around his neck and kissing him softly.

"Good, because it's the plan," he firmly tells me.

"There is food in the cupboards, and I just got some new movies," I say, rambling because I'm more nervous than I can cope with.

"Smile. Your parents will love to see you smile," he gently suggests and kisses me softly before letting me go. Leaning down, I stroke Amethyst before walking away to the front door. Just as I go to open it, someone knocks. I open the door to see Nikoli and Claus standing side by side.

"Hey," I say, smiling at them, which seems to shock them as I'm sure they expected to see me freaking out or something.

"Are you ready to go?" Nikoli asks, whereas Claus is silent. "The limo is waiting outside, and we are escorting you."

"Where is daddy dearest?" I sarcastically ask.

"Not dead, so who cares?" Nikoli coldly replies, nodding his head to the side. I walk with him, and Claus follows, but I don't dare look at him. I really, really have enough on my plate at the moment without letting him hurt me by being his usual self—which is an utter dickhead. The academy is unusually silent as we walk towards the doors and outside into the cold air. Mr. Bisgaard waits by the limo doors, and I can't read his expression until I'm right in front of him.

Sorrow. He feels sorry for me.

"Whatever may happen at the trial, I believe your parents have good souls," he tells me. "And your home is always here at The Demon Academy."

"I know they do," I reply. "And thank you."

"Good luck to your family, Miss Cameron. I will keep you in my thoughts," he tells me, and I nod once to him before getting in the limo, followed by Claus and Nikoli last who closes the door shut, and the limo drives off. I wish I could have seen Morgan before today; I know he would have made me feel safer somehow. Nikoli keeps his firm gaze set on me for a second before coming to sit at my side, and he pulls me to his chest. I wrap my arms around him and close my eyes, relaxing for just a second.

"Don't tell me it's going to be okay," I warn him.

"I won't. That would be a lie," he replies.

"Brutally honest, just how I like it," I chuckle.

"Always so strong, just why I love you," Nikoli replies, and Claus clears his throat.

"We will be here for you no matter—" Claus starts to say, but I don't want to hear it from him.

"Claus, you've made it perfectly clear you don't care about me," I reply.

"I'm good at acting, Lexi. I never once lied and told you I don't care," he all but growls.

"Then that just makes you more of a coward than I ever knew," I snap.

"Lexi, can we talk alone some time?" he asks me.

"No," I quickly reply.

"Lexi."

"Enough. Today is going to be difficult enough without you being a dickhead," Nikoli cuts in before kissing the top of my head. I lock eyes with Claus, because even though a part of me hates him...another part feels something else. I'm not admitting that I want him here or that I still love the idiot. I just can't see him walk out yet.

The rest of the journey to the demon leaders' building is silent, as no words could break the tension and fear that is thick in the air. I'm terrified of today, but I also really want to see my parents, and I know I will be finally able to. The limo soon comes to a stop, and Nikoli opens the door, climbing out first. I go to follow, but Claus catches my arm with his hand.

"I am here for you. I won't leave," he tells me.

"That will make a change," I retort, pulling my arm away from him and getting out of the limo. The wind blows against my face as I stand straight, looking up at the dozens of steps to the building where my parents await their trial. Where I found out I was a demon and my world was turned upside down. I just hope I won't be walking out of here heartbroken any time soon. We walk up the steps in silence, only the elements making any noise, but I hardly hear them over the beating of my heart.

At the top of the stairs is a man in an expensive suit, who looks about forty. His brown hair is touched with gray hairs, his blue eyes are familiar, and his arms are crossed. I know who he is without asking, simply because he looks so much like my mum.

"Hello, Uncle Harry," I say, stopping in front of him. He takes his time to look me over with a stern expression. "It's strange to meet you after reading your letters."

"Are you ready for today, niece?" he asks me, watching me ever so carefully. It hurts to look at him, he reminds me so much of my mum, and it's a reminder of all the secrets she never told me. He might be my uncle, but he is a stranger nonetheless. "Are you ready for any outcome? Your parents need to see you as their brave daughter; you cannot let them down. Understood?"

"Yes." As I do understand. It would hurt them to see me fall, just as it would hurt me to see them in pain.

I've learnt to be strong in the face of anything…now I have to see how strong I actually am.

CHAPTER

# TWENTY-ONE

DEATH BE A TRIAL TONIGHT...

My footsteps seem to echo with every step I take on the polished floors under my feet. I've walked this path before, but back then, I was confused and lost.

Now I am determined to save my parents, because I am not that girl who was kidnapped and taken. I will never be that girl again. If I am to stand a chance of helping my parents, I need to be strong and confident and play on the fact Lucifer thinks I'm the soon to be Queen of Hell. They won't kill my parents if they know I will never forget.

*I hope.*

The doors to the courtroom I was once in are

left open this time, with a row of Hellers standing in front of them. Going into the room, I see them straight away like there is no one else: my mum and dad. They are in chains, standing side by side, and they look tired, worn down but alive. A sob catches in my throat, and I step forward on instinct as Mum's blue eyes find mine, but my uncle catches my arm.

"Don't. You are a witness. You cannot speak to them until you have given your testimonial," he reminds me. I gulp and move my eyes to my dad, who is staring at me with his hazel eyes. My dad, wearing his sweater vest, his navy jeans and usually a pair of glasses, is a far cry from the man in a blue jumpsuit that is the same as the one my mother wears. My dad's brown hair, much like mine, is longer than usual and messy. My mum's brown hair has been cut short into a bob, and I wonder why she did that. I loved her long hair. "Come on," my uncle gently suggests, tugging on my arm to lead me to the bench where Nikoli and Claus are already sitting.

I sit down next to Claus, and my uncle sits at my side as I stare at my parents, trying to tell them how much I love them with just a look. I can't wait to hug them, to tell them how I wish they told me the truth but I forgive them for not anyway. I want to thank them for the normal upbringing I had, for showing how to be kind, and for always being there when I needed them. I want to tell them everything and nothing all at the same time. I just want them.

Hearing a seat being moved, I look up to see the leaders sitting down. I remember Magnus Belcher as the high leader, and he looks the same as he did the last time I saw him, red suit and all. I remember Maureen at his side, in a red dress with an even higher collar than the last one she wore. The other two council leaders are silent, near mirror images of when I saw them last. The doors slam shut just as Lucifer and Morgan walk into the room. Morgan walks over and sits next to my uncle, and I catch his gaze for just a second, long enough to know he is here for me. Lucifer all but prances into the room like the cruel asshole he is, before sitting in a throne seat in the middle of the room, where there is another chair in front of it. They are both made of red velvet and have high backs, with gold painted wooden arm rests.

"Welcome to the trial of Irene and Leo Cameron, charged with murdering five high demons and taking their souls. How do you both plead?" Magnus asks.

"Not guilty," both my mum and dad say at the same time, and I enjoy hearing their voices even under the circumstances.

"As expected. Now, you have not given an account of the night, but this is your chance. We will also hear from the witness, your own daughter," he replies.

"Tell me what happened to my souls," Lucifer asks, looking at my parents. They don't look at him, they look at me instead.

"Promise us you will not hurt Alexandria Cameron if we tell you the truth of that night," my dad asks Lucifer and the court. I want to tell them not to protect me, not if it means their lives, but I just know they won't listen. I got my stubbornness from them after all.

"We cannot make such promises," Magnus all but laughs. "How dare you make demands."

"I am not demanding you; this promise is for our king. Promise you will not kill her," my dad asks Lucifer, keeping his eyes on him the whole time.

"You have my word," Lucifer answers. "Now tell me where my souls are."

"We are sorry," Dad says to me, his eyes full of tears. "And for the record, it is my doing. My wife and daughter are innocent."

"No, Leo. We both made the choice," Mum interrupts.

"Enough, Irene," Dad harshly tells her before taking a deep breath. "On the night of the murders, we had a gathering for drinks and such. Something we did once a month, it was not unusual. Alexandria was a child, only seven years old, but it had happened a few times before. She opened a portal to hell itself, the worst part of hell, the prisons, where the demons are nothing but monsters. The first few times, she would close it so quickly nothing escaped, but this night, one monster did."

"Interesting. What creature of mine was released from the hell prisons?" Lucifer asks.

"I am unsure of the creature's true name, but it was deadly," Dad replies.

"Derek Mendoza was the one to kill it with Leo's help, as Lexi and I hid in the closet," Mum explains.

"This still doesn't explain where my souls are," Lucifer says, and he clearly only cares about one thing here.

"Lexi... she..." Dad hesitates.

"Out with it!" Magnus demands.

"I took the souls and sent them up into the light above me," I say, remembering it clearly. I stand up as the memory floods my mind like a movie I had forgotten. Or was made to forget. We came out of the closet, and the room was full of death and blood and souls. Green floating balls of light, and I reached a hand out to them, and they came to me. I remember how scared my parents were, but I thought it was about the dead people. "I can touch souls and stop them going down, and make them rise instead." The silence in the room is deafening as I remember everything, as my words echo around the room.

"Just like me. It is a power blessed only to two families of demons in the entire existence of, well, everything," Lucifer replies, though he sounds angry and dangerous. My palms sweat as everyone in the room just looks at me as I stand there.

"Then this is my fault. I should be the one that pays the price," I say, and my parents are not the only ones who shout in disagreement. Claus and Nikoli do as well.

"Quiet in my court, or you will all be

removed!" Maureen shouts, and the room goes silent. "Mr. and Mrs. Cameron, how can a lower demon have such a gift?"

"My family knew there was a chance we could inherit the gift. No one had the power until Lexi, as far as I know," my mum explains to her.

"That's why you were dumped on a church doorstep as children. Your true family wanted to hide you," Lucifer all but growls. "Very smart or dumb. I'm not sure which."

"Then you are innocent, and Alexandria is the one who committed the crime," Magnus replies.

"Let my parents go. I did this," I shout.

"As a child," Morgan interrupts me to say.

"Sit down, angel. You are not permitted to speak here," Magnus snaps.

"I will make the final choice," Lucifer replies.

"Lucifer...please. You promised not to hurt our child," Dad demands.

"I have chosen the verdict. As Alexandria Cameron was simply a child, she cannot be held accountable for her actions. Her parents are not accountable either," Lucifer says, and I sigh in relief, grinning at my parents. I mouth *I love you* to them as tears of happiness fall down my cheeks.

My happiness lasts all of two seconds. "But I find Leo and Irene Cameron guilty of hiding the true Queen of Hell from me for many years. That is a crime I will never forgive. The punishment is death."

"Punishment agreed. Death by holy fire," Magnus says, though I barely hear him as fear shocks me to the core.

"Make the girl leave the room," Maureen suggests as my shock turns into panic.

"I love you, baby girl!" Dad shouts to me.

"We will always be with you. Always," my mother says as Dad holds her close.

"NO!" I scream, jumping over the barrier and running to my parents. Lucifer catches me around the waist, holding me back as the world slows down. Magnus sends a stream of holy fire towards my parents, and I can't do anything but scream and beg for them to stop. The fire smothers them, and they cry out for me. I cry for them too, but no one helps.

No one can do anything.

My parents scream and scream with me as I

fall to my knees. Lucifer leans down to my side as I cry and plead for this all to be a dream.

"This is the punishment anyone will get if they dare to take you from me. Don't worry, dear sweet Alexandria, you will see their souls in hell very soon." I don't feel myself falling, but my body hits the ground, and I don't stop the darkness from taking me.

# CHAPTER
# TWENTY-TWO

FIVE IN THE BED, AND THE LITTLE ONE SAID...

I don't remember Nikoli carrying me out of the demon leaders' building and to the limo. I don't remember the words he whispered to me, or the hushed conversation between Claus and Morgan who came in the limo with us.

I didn't really take in anything as Nikoli took me into the academy and walked in my apartment, where in hushed whispers, Claus and Morgan tell a worried Javier what has happened. Now I blink my eyes one more time, tears still streaming down my cheeks as I stare up at the ceiling of my bed which I've been in for a long time. Hours likely.

"My parents are gone. Gone just like that, and I didn't get to say goodbye." Those were the words I said first before crying more, and Nikoli holds me even closer. I feel the bed dip as Morgan's hand finds mine, and another hand rests on my knee. Someone sits near my head, and I look up to see Javier, who moves so I can lie on his chest.

I just cry. I cry for my parents, the good people I know they were. I cry for all the moments in my life they will now miss. I cry for them and the pain they must have felt.

"Tell us something about your mum or dad. It might help to talk about the good memories rather than focusing on what happened today," Nikoli suggests.

"I don't know," I mutter.

"I had human parents who died at the same time as I did. When I was human, we owned a small boat, and as usual, on my eighteenth birthday, we went out to sea to celebrate. We got caught in a bad storm, and we all drowned in the same room. I don't focus on that moment when I saw them die just before I did myself, I focus on the way my mum laughed in joy when I passed my exams. I focus on the last football game my dad took me to, and how I hate football but never told him that. I have a million memories, just like you do. They, as well as us, will help piece your heart back together," Morgan tells me, strangely making me feel better.

"Once, my mum decided she would cook a meal for her and my dad's anniversary. But my mum can't cook, so I did the meal after she nearly burnt the flat down. I never said a word," I say, and I soon can't help but smile as I recount the memories I love the most. "At a local arcade, there was a machine with a purple cat teddy bear I really, *really* wanted, but I couldn't win it. I tried for weeks until I ran out of birthday money. Little did I know my dad had realised how much I wanted the teddy and somehow, he got it for me. I was ten years old, and I literally jumped into his arms and cried."

"No wonder you adopted Amethyst if you like cat teddies," Javier mutters. "I think a wolf teddy would be better."

"The imaginary cat you mean?" Claus asks, and I realise that he is sitting near the edge with his hand on my knee. I may slightly hate him, but for now he can stay.

"Amethyst isn't imaginary, and she has a real problem with walking in on me in the shower," Morgan comments with clear distaste. Smart kitty, I bet that is one hell of a view.

"I've never seen her," Nikoli comments.

"Me neither, bro," Claus replies.

"Maybe she just doesn't like demons. I always have her purring in my lap when I'm here," Javier replies.

"I'm slightly offended that your cat doesn't like me," Claus says, and I smile at him as the guys laugh. Even Morgan, to my surprise. I have four possessive, different raced, and usually aggressive as hell men in my bed, and they are all getting along like long lost friends.

"Are you hungry?" Javier asks me, stroking my hair in a soothing motion.

"Not really," I admit. "I miss them so much. All this time at the academy, I've told myself I will get my family back, and now they are just gone."

"You always will have them in your soul, but time will help, and I promise you won't be alone," Javier gently tells me.

"Never," Nikoli adds.

"I'm always here," Claus feels the need to say, and Morgan sighs.

"You couldn't get rid of me if you tried," Morgan creepily adds. Usually Nikoli is the creepy one, so it makes a nice change.

"This angel is creepy and your teacher. Can't you choose someone else?" Claus asks, and Morgan glares at him. "Joking, joking."

"Maybe we should have a funeral of sorts. A way for you to say goodbye," Nikoli suggests the idea.

"No," I quickly say.

"Why not?" Claus carefully asks. "You do need to say goodbye."

"Their souls are in hell, right?" I ask, and they all nod or murmur yes. "Then that means I can talk to them and say goodbye. I need that chance before I really accept they are gone."

"Whatever you need, we will do," Nikoli tell me.

"Except cook, I can't do that well," Claus jokes.

"Lucky I'm here then," Javier comments.

"I like to clean," Claus adds in. "It's pretty soothing."

"I'm not doing anything for the record," Morgan adds in, and I close my eyes as they chat between each other. Wherever you are, Mum and Dad, I will find your souls and say goodbye.

This is not the end.

# CHAPTER
# TWENTY-THREE
## A LETTER FROM THE DEAD

"You are acing necromancy like a god," Nikoli tells me, his arm wrapped around my waist as we walk towards my apartment. Thankfully, Lucifer never came back from the demon leaders' building, and it's given us some time to relax and for me to cope with the reality of my parents' death. I know I haven't accepted it, but being without them is actually something normal now at DA. I push the door to my apartment open and walk in to see my uncle standing by the window, holding a small white box.

"Uncle Harry, how did you get in here?" I ask.

"Through the door, how else?" Uncle Harry solemnly replies.

"Nikoli Lucifer," Nikoli says, walking up to my uncle and holding his hand out. They shake hands before Nikoli goes and sits down on the sofa, and I sit next to him. Uncle Harry sits in the chair and offers me the small white box he held.

"Your parents wrote this letter to you in secret, and I snuck it out of the building without anyone seeing it. There is also your mother and father's wedding rings in there and your mother's engagement ring. They are yours by right," he tells me, and I didn't even think about them. I look at the box. Knowing all that's left of my parents is in them is harder than I expected it to be. "If you're unluckily enough come to hell in the future, there is something for you there."

"Thank you," I shakily say, holding the box tightly.

"Do not thank me. I couldn't save my sister, and I doubt I will be able to save you, kid," he tells me, standing up. "I am returning to hell, and I hope to never see you there."

"You didn't kill them, Uncle Harry," I tell him, sensing his guilt is as bad as mine. That's all I can tell myself to cope with what happened. Lucifer killed them, and I am going to make him pay for it.

"I might as well have done," he tells me before walking out of the apartment, and the door slams shut behind him.

"Do you want me to leave?" Nikoli gently asks me.

"No, please don't," I say, looking into his eyes for a second before back to the box. I open the lid and pick up the three rings on top first. Uncle Harry has put them on a long silver chain, and I put the necklace on, letting the rings hang in the middle of my chest. I rub my thumb across the diamond of the engagement ring, like I did many times when the ring was on my mother's finger. I put the box to the side after taking the letter out and opening it up. It's hard to read it as tears burn my eyes, and I remind myself I need to read this.

*Our sweet baby girl,*

*We thought long about what to write here, as a simple apology for never telling you the truth is just not enough. We were scared to open you up to such a cruel world, but if you are reading this, that world has ended our lives.*

*We are sorry. We are so sorry for the life you must now walk alone.*

*We wanted to protect you, but that may be as impossible as we always suspected it was.*

*Your dad told you the truth. You belong to no one except yourself.*

*And that is the truth, please always remember it.*

*By now, you must be aware of the facts of your markings, and for answers, you must find a book that tells all tales. A race of fairy tales has the book, and you must find them and convince them to help you.*

*We love you so very much. So very, very much. Every second of our lives was made better when we had you.*

*Love your life, love your mates and everyone in your life.*

*Baby girl, we will never leave you. You can find us in your heart.*

*Love,*
*Mum and Dad*

I BURST INTO TEARS, and Nikoli pulls me onto his lap, holding me closely as I finally admit what I didn't want to before.

*My parents are gone.*

## CHAPTER
# TWENTY-FOUR
WHY DON'T STUBBORN BOYS SAY SORRY?

"You look mad as hell today," Lela comments as I watch Claus laugh with Morgan in the middle of my survival basics class. I'm sick and tired of this hot and cold game Claus is playing with me, but I don't tell her that. For the last few weeks, Claus has been kind to me when he feels like it, but he avoids any serious conversation that I try to have. He watches me as much as I watch him, both of us knowing damn well that we are destined mates, but I won't give in until he says sorry.

And he won't say flipping sorry. The stubborn asshat. I know he wants to; I can see it every time he looks at me.

And it's been weeks. Thankfully, Lucifer hasn't come back to the academy, because I'm half likely to attempt killing him. Morgan says we should leave as soon as Gabriel finds us somewhere safe to go. Apparently, he hasn't found anywhere yet, and the longer we stay here, the more dangerous it becomes.

"Who wants to fight against Claus? The theme of today's class is holy fire," Morgan asks, and there is silence.

"I will," I stand up, and the room goes silent.

"Damn, girl," Lela whispers under her breath, and Morgan only smiles. He knows how good I've gotten at controlling holy fire in the weeks we have been training. Claus only smirks as I move to stand in front of him.

"Everyone else can run five laps around the academy. As we all know, holy fire is dangerous, and though this room is protected, we best not test our endurance of holy fire today," Morgan instructs, clapping his hands, and everyone all but runs out of the room, followed by Morgan who pauses in the doorway, his voice laced with humour. "Don't kill him, Miss Cameron."

"The angel has too much confidence in a new lower demon," Claus mutters.

"Seems you don't know me at all, Claus Lucifer," I say, and I close my eyes. When I open them, holy fire is streaming out of my hands in spinning tunnels which twirl around my body and fly around the room. Claus steps back, but I direct the tunnels to swirl around him, boxing him in like a caged animal.

"Your eyes glow when you do this," he calmly comments. "It's beautiful. You're beautiful."

"Fight me back," I demand.

"No," he simply replies, and I make the holy fire move closer to him, not hurting but enough to make him sweat. "I'm scared of losing you. That's the truth behind everything."

"You have to have me to lose me, Claus," I snap.

"Lucifer has taken everything good from my life except for my brother. I don't know why I fooled myself that you would be safe from him, but I did. Then he took you from me," he tells me.

"He didn't take me. I am not his," I say. "I will never be."

"But he will never let you go," Claus reminds me.

"Claus, if you won't fight for us, then what is the point in this?" I ask. "Love isn't easy, it never is. Walking away shouldn't be this easy for you, and I will never chase you. Claus, you have to make a choice, and I will understand either way."

"I'm sorry, and I love you," he tells me, and anger fills me. He can't just say that. I slam the holy fire into his chest, and he flies across the room, smacking into the wall. I know the holy fire can't hurt him, not with his angel blood, but hopefully the wall hurt a bit. I storm over to him as he stands up, and he grins even as blood trickles down the cut on his forehead to his cheek.

"You don't get to say sorry and tell me you love me to fix everything! You abandoned me when I needed you! You left me alone with your crazy dad! How could you do that to me?" I say, and I slam my fists into his chest. He grabs my arms and pulls me to him, kissing me harshly and spinning us around so my back presses against the wall.

"I'm sorry. I fucked up," he whispers against my lips. "You're right, I'm a coward and I've never fought for anything in my life. I want to fight for you, Lexi. I've made that decision."

"Don't kiss me like that," I protest, pushing him away, but he doesn't move an inch. Damn demon.

"Why?" he demands, lifting his arms and placing them next to my head, boxing me in so I can only see and feel Claus, nothing but Claus.

"You kiss me like I'm yours, but all you do is walk away! You won't fight for us, you won't even try for what we could have. Yet you kiss me like my soul belongs to you and you won't take anything less!" I almost scream, feeling more than frustrated. "Just let me go. For real this time. Can't you see that all you are doing is hurting me?"

"I can't let you go…" he softly tells me. "It's because, despite what all the magic in the fucking world says, you are mine."

"Then prove it, and don't you ever walk away from me again." And he kisses me, a kiss that goes a long way to proving one thing: Claus Lucifer belongs to me.

# CHAPTER
# TWENTY-FIVE

MAY THE TRUE ALPHA RULE.

JAVIER

"Son, this is Emerald—"

"Just go, you aren't my mate, and we both know it," I tell the poor girl who looks at me with doe eyes and blushed cheeks. There is only one woman who is my mate, and she never looks at me like I'm nothing more than a pretty face. Half the time, she looks like she wants to kill me, and the other, well I like the other emotion. The girl walks out of the throne room in tears, and I cross my arms, arching an eyebrow at my father.

"Everyone get out," my father roars, and his betas quickly leave the room, leaving only me and my father in here. He leans back in his seat, stretching his legs out and placing his head in his hands before meeting my eyes. He looks tired. So fucking tired. "I know you love the demon, I'm not a fool. I loved Sera's mother before I mated your mother. Did you know that?"

"No. Why did you mate my mother then?" I ask, not used to my father telling me any real emotions.

"Because she was a suitable mate for an alpha wolf. Sera's mother was human, the daughter of a butcher, and she had nothing. I loved her more than myself, and a part of me died when your mother killed her. It was my fault, I should have left her for the good of everyone," he tells me.

"Do you regret your actions?" I ask.

"No. I have you, and that wouldn't have happened if I did anything different. I love you, son, but your love for this demon needs to stop," he tells me, but I don't believe him. My father never loved me, not really, or he doesn't know how to. I lived a childhood of being shaken awake every morning at five a.m. and then running for hours. Even if I threw up, even if I was sick, I had to run. Then I would hunt for my food to show my worth as alpha, and then the evening was spent with teachers learning about the world I can never escape. That isn't love.

"You can't just stop loving someone, father," I explain to him.

"I know that. I didn't ask for that; I am asking for you to walk away from her," he tells me. "I'm telling you to."

"I will never do that," I say, making a stand. I should have kissed Lexi in front of the pack and fought for her. I should have never let her dance with my father and not me.

She is mine. And I am hers.

Which means the pack can't have me too.

"You will give up your blood right for a pretty demon?" he roars, standing up off his throne. "Have you lost your god damn mind?!"

"I will give up everything I am if that is what she needs of me. Her name is Alexandria Cameron, father, and she is my wolf marked mate," I tell him, holding my head high.

"NO!" he shouts, his voice half a growl. I brace myself to shift just as the doors are slammed open and Eike strides in, covered in blood and fur. And naked. I see the guards on the ground outside, covered in their own blood. Eike looks dangerous and determined.

"Eike Matthews, what are you doing in here?" my father demands. "How fucking dare you kill my guards and walk in here."

"I have come to challenge you for alpha. The alpha bloodline runs in my blood, and it is mine. Javier, I presume you do not want it?" Eike asks me, and for the first time, I'm fucking proud of my best friend. Eike has kept his wolf at bay with alcohol and girls to distract from the fact that he is a born alpha. His ancestors ran this pack for hundreds of years, and all that power rests in Eike. He is the true alpha, hidden away. My place was always with Lexi.

"No," I answer.

"Javier…" my father's heartbroken plea hurts, but I stand tall. This isn't what I want, and it never has been.

"Do you accept my challenge?" Eike asks, and I walk backwards until I am out of the way. My father doesn't answer, but he shifts into his large wolf, and Eike does the same. Not many have seen Eike shift, considering he never does, but I smile when I see Eike's huge gray wolf. The wolf towers over my father's, and with a clash of teeth and fur, they crash into each other. The fight is brutal and cruel. Blood and fur scatters everywhere, and growls fill the throne room. I watch until it becomes clear my father is losing, and Eike's wolf gets hold of my father's neck between his teeth and holds him down. Eike's eyes meet mine, and I nod. It has to be done; my father is no angel. I look into my father's eyes as Eike fatally bites into his neck and lets him drop to the floor. My father shifts back, and I walk over as Eike shifts too. I kneel down as my father dies, and he reaches a hand out, covering mine.

"L-ov-e is d-ea-d-ly..." I watch him die, and close my eyes for a brief second. Even dying, he couldn't say he supported me.

"Javier—" Eike gently says.

"Alpha Eike," I answer.

"Fuck off, you don't call me that. You are my brother and my beta," he tells me, offering me a hand. I grab his hand and stand up before patting his bloody shoulder.

"I'm proud of you, but I can't be your beta," I admit. "My place isn't with the pack anymore."

"You need to get the girl. I have a similar mission in mind as well," he tells me. "After sorting the pack out, of course."

"Who?" I ask. I didn't know Eike ever liked anyone.

"Who do you think?" he replies, and I frown. "She is the only girl that tells me I'm an asshole, and I fucking love it." If he means my sister, I'm going to—

"No!" my mother screams as she walks into the throne room, followed by my sister and five guards. They hold my sister's arms as my mother runs in, falling to her knees and covering my father's body. I don't know why she bothers fake crying; everyone knows she never loved my father.

*And he never loved her.*

"Alpha...Eike. We found Serafin Luque trying to escape the pack," the guards say.

"Lexi needs us!" Sera explains.

"Unless you want your heads removed, let her the fuck go. Now," Eike demands, and I cross my arms as he storms over as they let Sera go. She stares, an empty stare, at our father on the floor. "I am alpha now, pass the message around. Anyone touches Serafin or Javier, and they are challenging me. Now get out of my house."

"This is my house. My house!" my mother wails.

"This was never your house, mother. It was a prison that has finally ended," I say. "And technically, Eike's ancestors built the whole pack, so it is his."

"And you need to leave," Eike adds in. I don't look at her as I walk to my sister and pull her into my arms as she cries for the father that never truly loved her. He pretended to, but I think he only loved the parts of Sera that reminded him of her mother. Sera was nothing to him in the end, and we all knew it.

Love is deadly; father was right, but what he didn't know is that it is worth fighting for.

# CHAPTER
# TWENTY-SIX

## THE TIME THE ANGEL MET THE WOLF

"About time," Nikoli says as he leans against the wall by the door to my apartment, his arms crossed and his eyes on my hand linked with Claus's.

"He isn't completely forgiven, but he has one chance," I explain.

"That I'm never going to fuck up," Claus tells me, kissing my cheek.

"You best not. I'm going to use holy fire on something other than your hair if you do," I warn him.

"I will help you if he does," Nikoli half jokingly adds. "But we have something far more serious to talk about. Inside." I don't need to ask Nikoli how serious, his tone says it all, and considering everything going on, we quickly follow Nikoli inside. Claus shuts the door as I follow Nikoli into the kitchen area. He stops and walks to me, taking my hands.

"Daddy dearest is back," Nikoli says the second Claus walks in. "And he demanded I come here to get you to see him. Seems like he is sorry."

"Sorry doesn't cut it. He killed my parents for simply protecting their child," I say, wishing I was strong enough to kill him.

"I know. That's why I called Javier," Nikoli says. "But I talked to Sera instead. She is going to find him."

"You have Javier's number?" I ask.

"Who is Javier?" Claus interjects. Ah yeah, I don't think they have met yet.

"A wolf in love with Lexi. We all have a lot to catch up on, but that isn't important right now. Right now, you need to pack some clothes and anything you want to keep. You're leaving tonight—" Nikoli says, but I interrupt him.

"No, not without Morgan, and we have to stay for now," I say.

"Why?" he asks.

"An angel friend of his is going to find somewhere for us to hide. A place your dad can't find any of us," I explain.

"Why would an angel help you?" Claus asks.

"I trust you, so I'm telling you both this. I have an angel blessing on my thigh and a wolf mark on my arm from Javier's wolf," I explain. "Oh, and two horse marks that appeared after... well, after stuff." My cheeks are red as Nikoli chuckles.

"She means sex," Nikoli fills in.

"Ah right. Horse marks appearing after sex. That's a new one," Claus mutters, rubbing his neck. "Holy shit, this is complicated," he says, rubbing the back of his neck harder. "I don't think there has ever been a demon with an angel mark. Then again, I've never heard of the choosing stone showing anyone as a queen before."

"Have you two held the stone?" I ask, wanting to change the subject.

"No, never," Nikoli answers.

"We are going to tell Lucifer that you are sick with a cold or some shit. We will distract him, and you can tell your wolf that you aren't leaving," Claus suggests. I doubt Lucifer will believe that though.

"Any chance you have Morgan's number? We should group chat us all, save us passing on conversations," Nikoli says.

"A group chat with three demons, an angel and a wolf. Sounds like fun," Claus jokes, and I grin.

"Pack a bag, just in case," Nikoli suggests, briefly kissing me before walking to the door. Claus presses a gentle kiss on my cheek before walking out with his brother.

"Am?" I shout for her as I go to my bedroom and turn on the lights. She isn't here, I soon figure out, and I quickly pack a bag full of clothes, the letters from my parents, and my uncle's necklace that somehow appeared on my bed one day. Not that I wear it now, knowing what it is. I'm packing some cat food as the door to my apartment is opened, and I tense up, wondering if it is Lucifer, before I see black angel wings and then Morgan's stern expression. He walks right up to me and kisses me. A full kiss, not holding anything back as he lifts me onto the kitchen counter and parts my legs, pulling me against his body. I'm sure I hear the door being slammed, but I'm so lost in the way Morgan is kissing me that I don't move. That is until I hear a low growl that gives me goose bumps and gets Morgan's attention.

"Angel, aren't you meant to be her teacher?" Javier asks as Morgan turns around, and I jump off the cabinet side with flushed cheeks.

"What can I say, I'm a bad fucking teacher. You must be the wolf," Morgan replies, holding an arm out to block me behind his back, overprotecting me.

"You must be the angel," Javier sternly replies. Talk about a tense situation.

"Is it always this awkward here?" Eike drones, and I hear Sera's giggle as I push Morgan's arm away and step around him. Javier is in a stare down with Morgan as Sera comes to me and hugs me tightly, whispering in my ear.

"I'm so sorry about your parents. I'm so, so sorry, Lexi." I nod against her shoulder, not really having the strength to reply to her as a sob catches in my throat. Sera has a thick black cloak on, the same as Eike and Javier. I see under the cloaks, they all have casual clothes. Sera's hair is up in a messy bun, and her eyes are nothing but happy to see me. I'm pulled from Sera into Javier's embrace, and I wrap my arms around his neck, resting my head on his chest for a moment.

"I don't believe we have really met. I'm Serafin, and this is Eike. I'm sure you've heard of Javier," Sera says.

"It is good to officially meet you, Serafin," Morgan comments. "Now, why are you all here?"

"Lexi is leaving," Javier says as he lets me go.

"I agree," Morgan states.

"What about Gabriel?" I ask him.

"I don't want you in the academy with Lucifer, not now he is back. We can find a way to contact Gabriel when we are hidden," Morgan suggests.

"So we are doing this?" I quietly ask, and they all nod. "Wait, I can't find Amethyst. I can't leave without her."

"I will search for her, but you need to leave first with the wolves," Morgan tells me.

"Why? What are you going to do?" I catch Morgan's arm, and he takes my hand off, lifting it to his lips and gently kissing the back.

"I'm going to make sure Lucifer isn't going to follow us any time soon," Morgan tells me.

"I will help," Javier states, nodding at Morgan. Javier kisses me on the cheek before letting me go, and my heart feels like it's in my stomach as I watch Javier hug Sera and pat Eike on the shoulder. "You two take Lexi to where we talked about. Eike, I'm trusting you with the most important people in my life. You got this?"

"I will protect Lexi and your sister with my life," Eike tells him. "An alpha's promise." *Wait, alpha?*

"Good. If anything happens to them, you better pray you are dead, wolf," Morgan darkly promises. Javier pats a nervous looking Eike on the shoulder before following Morgan out of the apartment.

"Are you ready to leave?" Sera gently asks.

"I have been since the first moment I got here," I tell her, and she grins.

"There's nothing like escaping, Lexi." I pray she is right. I pray the devil can't find us, because if he does, we are dead.

# CHAPTER
# TWENTY-SEVEN
### THE DEMON CAT.

MORGAN

"Which way?" the wolf asks me as we step out of the elevator into the empty reception hall. I immediately go on alert at the sight of no Hellers guarding the doors and the silence found up here. The wolf picks up on my tension as he looks to me, and I nod once, my eyes saying everything.

Something is wrong. And right now, we don't need that. Walking across the entrance hall, my footsteps sound like rocks smashing against the tiles in the silence, whereas the wolf is almost silent in his movement. I push the doors open to Lucifer's apartment and head in, but I don't find Lucifer. I find his sons instead, just as they are heading out.

"What are you two doing here?" they ask at the same time. It's creepy.

"Looking for Lucifer," I reply.

"Same as us then. He is gone," Nikoli answers. "Where is Lexi?"

"With my sister and a wolf I trust. The new alpha," Javier says, and all of us are silent for a moment.

"Where would he go?" Claus mutters.

"After Alexandria," a voice I don't know says, and I turn around to see Alexandria's cat, Amethyst, sitting in the middle of the entrance hall.

"Fuck no. How are you here?" Claus angrily demands, stepping around me.

"That's Lexi's cat, Amethyst. Why are you mad?" I ask.

"That's no fucking cat," Nikoli snaps. "How could we have been so stupid not to realise?"

"Come on, mother. Cat got your tongue?" Claus asks, and I stare in shock. Amethyst is their mother? How does that fucking work? I knew demons are messed up bastards, but this is a little extreme.

"I know you hate me, but Alexandria needs your help. Lucifer is going after her," Amethyst says, almost pleading.

"The cat is a person? Your mother?" Javier asks the crazy question before I can.

"The cat is a demon cursed to a cat form. She can only shift back into her mortal form once a month for a few minutes. Our father cursed her after she killed our foster parents," Nikoli explains. Ah, this ball of crazy makes more sense now.

"Everyone meet Lilith. That's her real name," Claus spits out.

"We don't have time to talk about this—" Lilith starts to say.

"I'm sure Lexi won't agree. You've been lying to her for years!" Nikoli shouts at the...cat. It's weird.

"Because her parents asked me to watch her. I've done nothing but protect Lexi, and you two do not know everything," the cat replies. It's strange to see a cat talking, it really, really is.

"Bullshit. You are selfish and cruel!" Nikoli

shouts. "And Lexi is going to hate you as much as we do."

"Enough!" I shout. "Lexi, where would she be right now?"

"I can lead you to her. Her parents gave me her blood years ago to help control her powers and so I can find her at any time," Lilith tells me. It still freaks me out that this isn't a cat and she saw me in the shower lots of times.

"This just gets better and better," I say.

"Show us the way, cat," Javier frustratedly growls.

"You were always my favourite, wolf," Lilith purrs before running to the lift. God help us, we are following a cat who is actually the consort of hell.

## CHAPTER
# TWENTY-EIGHT

DEATH IS JUST THE BEGINNING...

None of us talk much as we climb across the rocks on the cliff to another ledge. Eike and Sera have wolf senses, so they are much better at this climbing stuff than I am. Sera stays in front of me, but Eike stays behind as we get onto a long pathway carved into the cliff. The pathway leads deeper into the cliff, and I sigh a little breath of relief from being away from the edge.

"Eike is alpha now," Sera tells me, looking back with a big grin. "Told you he could do it."

"Congrats!" I turn back to tell Eike, only to see his eyes turn from relaxed to fearful and in pain. Everything in the world slows down as I turn back, just as Lucifer stabs a sword through

Sera's stomach. I scream as Eike's wolf jumps over my head, crashing into Lucifer, and they both tumble off the cliff. I catch Sera as she falls to the rock, her head landing on my lap.

"No, no, no. Not you. I can't lose you too," I mumble as tears fall down my cheeks, landing in her hair. She gasps for air as hot blood pours into my lap, and I cup her face, tilting her to see me. Her eyes look like they are fading already as she gasps for air, and her skin goes a sickly pale. Oh god no. I can't lose her. I flipping can't.

"Goodbye, my best friend. I really do love you, Lexi," she tells me before coughing on the blood in her mouth, and her head rolls to the side in my arms.

"God, no. No, please no!" I plead and scream as I lay her down on the stone and start trying to bring her back, pressing down on her chest even though I know she is dying. She is leaving me. Suddenly, a bright green light, shaped like a star, floats out of her chest, and I reach out, grabbing the edge. Another hand grabs the other side and tries to pull it from me, though I don't let go. I meet Lucifer's eyes over what I think is Sera's soul, and he smirks.

"The half breed wolf's soul belongs to me,"

he growls. A big wave crashes sea water across us, but I never let go, not as lightning flashes across the sky and lights up the devil's evil grin.

"Her soul does not belong to you. It's too good, too pure. I will never let you have her!" I shout at him.

"How inviting you are, fighting for the weak," he muses, like this is nothing. To him, it might not be.

"How fucked-up you are, fighting for a mate who wants to kill you!" I shout at him. "And I promise you, Lucifer, I will kill you one day. I will end your life."

"I will make you a deal. You can have this soul and place it back in this body. I will heal her for you, and then you will come to hell with me, willingly, and become my mate in a ceremony there," he suggests, a deal he knows I want part of. The devil whispers exactly what I want, and my hand shakes on Sera's soul as I look down at her dead body, her glazed eyes.

"Deal," I promise, and I know I've given away something I never should have. For Sera, I will pay the price.

Sera deserves to live more than anyone I know, even if it damns my soul.

I promised her brother I would keep her alive. I promised myself no one else I love would die because of me.

This way, I keep all my promises even at the cost of my soul. Lucifer's smile is too wide, so happy as he lets Sera's soul go, and I grab it with both hands, holding it closely as he pulls the sword out of Sera's chest. Lucifer's hands glow red as he hovers them over Sera's wound for only a moment before stepping back. I push the soul into Sera's chest, and I watch as she slowly gasps, blinking her eyes open. I wipe my tears away as I stand up, and Lucifer steps over Sera to me. He holds his hand out to our left, just over the cliff, and orange fire burns into the air.

"Jump into the fire with me, my mate. And we will forever burn." Without looking back, I let the devil grab my arm and drag me into hell.

# EPILOGUE

Lucifer's arm wraps so tightly around me as we free fall into the dark, burning tunnel that leads right down into hell. The heat is so hot it feels like it's burning every inch of my body, and I can smell nothing but smoke. I see the edge of the portal above as it starts to close, leaving the people I care about on the other side. At least they will be safe. Lucifer's deep, terrifying laugh fills my ears.

He won.

I gasp, reaching my hands up in the air as Morgan flies through the portal, and he screams in pain. He screams so loudly as his wings burn away into nothing but embers, and bright red light shines from every part of his body. He is frozen in the middle of the air for a brief second, and I realise he has done something for me he never, *ever* should have done.

He is a fallen angel now.

*No.*

*For the second time in history, an angel fell into hell for a demon he loved...for the fallen never rise again.*

Keep reading with Savage as Hell

# NOTE FROM THE AUTHOR.

Hello my lovely readers.

Thank you, thank you, thank you!! I hope you enjoyed the second part to The Demon Academy Series. Book three, Savage as Hell, is on pre-order. Don't worry, that won't be the end of this world. Starting next year, there will be a series called The Angel Academy that follows this world a few years later.

A big thank you to my family and everyone that supported me with this book! Thank you to my wonderful Pack Leaders for everything. <3

Frani Nickerson, thank you, for naming one special cat in this series.

You're all amazing and I couldn't do this without you guys.

I've added an excerpt at the end of this book from another academy series of mine called Wings of Ice. This book is an academy full of dragons and a complete five book series!

Happy Reading!! G. xoxo

# About G. Bailey

G. Bailey is a USA Today and international bestselling author of books that are filled with everything from dragons to pirates. Plus, fantasy worlds and breath-taking adventures.

G. Bailey is from the very rainy U.K. where she lives with her husband, two children, three cheeky dogs and one cat who rules them all.

(You can find exclusive teasers, random giveaways and sneak peeks of new books on the way in Bailey's Pack on Facebook or on TIKTOK — gbaileybooks)

Find more books by G. Bailey on Amazon...
Link here.

# More Books by G. Bailey

Her Guardians Series

Her Fate Series

Protected By Dragons Series

Lost Time Academy Series

The Demon Academy Series

Dark Angel Academy Series

Shadowborn Academy Series

Dark Fae Paranormal Prison Series

Saved By Pirates Series

The Marked Series

HOLLY OAK ACADEMY SERIES

THE ALPHA BROTHERS SERIES

A DEMON'S FALL SERIES

THE FAMILIAR EMPIRE SERIES

FROM THE STARS SERIES

THE FOREST PACK SERIES

THE SECRET GODS PRISON SERIES

THE REJECTED MATE SERIES

FALL MOUNTAIN SHIFTERS SERIES

ROYAL REAPERS ACADEMY SERIES

THE EVERLASTING CURSE SERIES

THE MOON ALPHA SERIES

**Four Dragon Guards. Three Curses. Two Heirs. One Choice...**
**Forbidden love or the throne of the dragons?**

Isola Dragice thought she knew what her future would bring. Only, one earth-shattering moment destroys everything.

When war threatens her home, Isola returns from earth to the world of dragons she knows nothing about, and to Dragca Academy. When the four most powerful dragon guards in history are ordered to protect her, they didn't expect to be protecting an accident prone princess. One who, accidentally, nearly kills her whole class at Dragca Academy in her first week.

*What happens when fire falls for Ice?*

18+ **Reverse harem romance**

Book One of Five.

# BONUS READ OF WINGS OF ICE

Everything inside me screams as I run through the doors of the castle, seeing the dead dragons lining the floors, the view making me sick to my stomach. I try not to look at the spears in their stomachs, the dragon-glass that is rare in this world. *Where did they get it?* The more and more bodies I pass, both dragon and guards, the less hope I have that my father is okay. *No, I can't be too late, I can't lose him, too.* The once grand doors to the throne room are smashed into pieces of stone, in a pile on the floor, and only the hinges to the door still hang on the walls. I run straight over, climbing over the rocks and broken stone. The sight in front of me makes me stop, not believing what I'm seeing, but I know it's true.

"Father . . .?" I plead quietly, knowing he won't reply to me. My father is sitting on his throne, a sword through his stomach, and an open-mouthed expression on his face. His blood drips down onto the gold floors of the throne room, and snow falls from the broken ceiling onto his face. There's no ice in here, no sign he even tried to fight before he was killed. He must not have seen it coming; he trusted whoever killed him.

"No," is all I can think to say as I fall to my knees, bending my head and looking down at the ground instead of at the body of my father. *I couldn't stop this, even after he warned me and risked everything.* I hear footsteps in front of me as I watch my tears drip onto the ground, but I don't look up. I know who it is. I know from the way they smell, my dragon whispers to me their name, but I can't even think it.

"Why?" I ask, even as everything clicks into place. I should have known; I should have never trusted him.

"Because the curse has to end. Because he was no good for Dragca. Our city needs a true heir, me. I'm the heir of fire and ice, the one the prophecy speaks of, and it's finally time I took what is mine," he says, and every word seems to cut straight through my heart. *I trusted him.*

"The curse hasn't ended, I'm still here," I whisper to the dragon in front of me, but I know he can hear my words as if I had just spoken them into his ear.

"Not for long, not even for a moment longer, actually. Your dragon guard will only thank me when you are gone. I didn't want to do this to you, not in the end, but you are too powerful. You are of no use to me anymore, not unless you're gone," he says. I look down at the ground as his words run around my head, and I don't know what to do. I feel lost, powerless, and broken in every way possible. There's a piece of the door in front of me that catches my attention, a part with the royal crest on it. The dragon in a circle, a proud, strong dragon. My father's words come back to me, and I know they are all I need to say.

"There's a reason ice dragons hold the throne and have for centuries. There is a reason the royal name Dragice is feared," I say and stand up slowly, wiping my tears away.

"We don't give up, and we bow to no one. I'm Isola Dragice, and you will pay for what you have done," I tell him as I finally meet his now cruel eyes, before calling my dragon and feeling her take over.

## CHAPTER 29
# BONUS READ

Monsters are everywhere.

The monster in front of me twists its grotesque head, assessing me with its red eyes and mottled skin. It stands at over seven feet, two feet taller than me, and its once mortal-like body is a mixture of wolf and gods know what else. I risk taking my eyes off it for a second to look for my partner, and I catch a flash of red in the darkness behind the monster. I block out the awful stench of the creature and the rattling noise of its bones as it moves while I look for a safe way to take it down without getting us killed.

Clenching my magically blessed dagger in my hand, I whistle loudly. The monster roars loud enough to shake the derelict walls of the ruins before barrelling for me, each step shaking the ground. Like the dumbass that I am, I don't run but charge right back at it to meet it halfway. This plan better work, or I'm so fired. Or dead. I'm not sure which is worse.

"Calliophe! To your left!"

I barely hear my partner's warning shout before something hard rams into the side of me, shooting me into the air. I crash into the stone wall, all the air leaving my lungs as I roll to the floor and gasp in pain.

That hurt.

Blood fills my mouth as I push myself up and pause as I get a look at the giant cat-like thing in front of me. It might have once been a cat, even an exotic and expensive breed, but now it's been warped and changed like the monster behind it. It might even have been his pet. Once.

It lunges for me, snapping a row of sharp yellow teeth, and I narrowly jump to the side before kicking it with my boot. It hisses as I grapple for my dagger in the dust and slash the air between us as a warning as I crouch down. Its eyes are like yellow puddles of water, and I can see my reflection. Despite being covered in dust and dirt, my pink eyes glow slightly, and I look tiny in comparison. Even tiny, with a dagger, can be deadly. If the main monster runs, we might not get another chance to catch it for days, so I call to it, "Over here!"

The strange cat hisses once more, and the hair on its back rises. It straightens with its five strange legs that make it almost as tall as a dog.

A pain-filled female grunt echoes to me, and I clench my teeth. "I need a little help over here, Calli! Or I'm singing and screwing us both over!"

Dammit. I'm going to be the one buying the drinks tonight if she sings. Or worse, explaining this messed up mission to our boss. I'd rather buy the whole entire bar drinks and be poor. I jump on the cat, surprising it and slamming my dagger into its throat as it scratches and bites me before it goes still in my arms. I gently lower it to the ground, closing my eyes for a moment. I love animals, but whatever that was, death was a mercy for it. I pull my dagger out of it, yellow sticky blood dripping down my hand as I run across the ruins to Nerelyth. Somehow, she has gotten herself under a large piece of stone barely propped against a wall where she's hiding, and the monster is on top of it, clawing at the gap and nearly squishing her. I see her wave her arm at me from the small gap, and I sigh. There is only one way to capture a monster. Get up close and personal, and hope it doesn't eat me.

Thankfully, with Nerelyth's distraction, the monster's back is to me as I pull out my enchanted rope and let it wrap around my leg as I run across the ruins and close the gap between us, keeping my footsteps silent. Nerelyth's eyes widen when she spots me, but I don't pause as I leap off a fallen ledge and land on the creature's back, grunting at the impact on my swollen ribs, but my dagger easily slides into its back. Its skin is like goo, and I struggle to hold on as it straightens with a roar, but I lasso my rope around its neck with my other hand. The monster almost screams like a mortal as I let go, sliding down the monster's back and landing in a heap on the ground. I crawl backwards as the rope magically wraps itself over and over around the monster until it ties its legs together and it falls to the side. The rope won't kill it, but it will stay locked up like this for hours, depending on how good the enchantment is.

With a grunt, I stand up and wipe the goo off my hands and walk over to where Nerelyth is still hiding. I tilt my head and look down at my partner, who has her eyes closed. "It's sorted now."

Nerelyth is lying face up under the stone, her red hair splayed around her. Her chest is moving fast as she finally opens her eyes and looks over at me, arching an eyebrow. "Thank you. Again," I tell her. "We might have fucked up." I offer her my hand as she brushes the dust off her leather clothes. "Any chance you love me for saving you and you will explain it to the boss?"

"Not a chance," she chuckles as I help her climb out, light shining in from the bright sun hanging over us. We both stop to look over at the monster, who is trying to escape the rope. "Third one this month. Where do you think they are coming from?"

"Not a clue," I mutter, eyeing the monster suspiciously. "I'm not sure M.A.D. even knows where the hybrids are coming from. They still happily send us out with no warning that this wasn't a normal job. Assholes."

She shrugs a slender shoulder, picking out flecks of dust from her flawless waist-length dark red hair that matches the red curls of water marks around her cheek that go all the way down her neck to her back. I'm certain I look much worse than she does, and I'm not even attempting to take my hair out of my braid to fix it. "The money is worth it."

Lie. I've been in the Monster Acquisitions Division, aka M.A.D., for three years, and the pay has never been good compared to the other divisions, and we both know it. Like everyone says, you have to be literally mad to make it in M.A.D. for more than a month.

Most enforcers, like us, are sent here as a punishment for fucking up. I had no choice but to take this job, as it was all I could get with my background, lack of money, and young age when I started at only eighteen. I glance at my partner of just one year and wonder again why a siren is working in one of the shittiest divisions in Ethereal City. Sirens are one of the wealthiest races, and the few I know work at the top of the enforcers. Not at the bottom, like us, which makes me question my friend's motives for being here with me once again. "Drinks tonight?"

"You know it," she says with a friendly smile and tired viridescent green eyes. "I'll send a Flame to get some enforcers down here to take him in. You get back to the office and good luck."

I groan and send a silent prayer to the dragon goddess herself to save me.

I HEAD across the busy market street and look up at the Enforcer Headquarters as I stand on the sidewalk. The streets around me are filled with mortals and supernaturals heading to or from the bustle of the market to buy wares, food or nearly anything they want. The market hill is right at the top of the city, and it's the biggest market in Ethereal City. Fae horses wait by their owners' carts at the side of the main path, and I eye a soft white horse nearby for a moment and admire its shiny coat.

From this point, I can see nearly all of Ethereal City, from the elaborate seven hundred and four skyscrapers right down to the emerald green sea and the circular bay at the bottom of the city. Ethereal City was created over two thousand years ago, and the bay is even older than that. Dozens, if not hundreds, of ships line the ports, and they look like sparkling silver lines on the crystal green sea. Beyond that, the swirling seas of the largest lake in the world stretch all the way to the horizon and far beyond.

Most of Wyvcelm is this land, wrapped around the jeweled seas between Ethereal City and Goldway City on the other side. There are a few islands off the mainland, and one of them I want to go to one day—when I'm rich enough. Junepit City, the pleasure lands. I shake my head, pushing away that dream to focus on the Jeweled Seas, and I think of Nerelyth every time I see it.

The Jeweled Seas are ruled by the Siren King, and no one ever travels through them unless you are a siren, escorted by sirens, or want to die. Nerelyth told me once about how going through the fast, creature-filled rapids and the narrow cliff channels makes it nearly impossible to survive for long unless you know the way and can control the water. Above the sea level is worse as enchanted tornadoes reach high into the sky, swirling constantly over the waters controlled by the sirens themselves. That's why they're one of the richest races in Wyvcelm, because if the sirens didn't control the tornadoes, they would rip into both Ethereal City and Goldway City, ending thousands of lives. But they are not richer than the fae who rule over our lands and pay them to keep us safe.

I turn to my right, looking up at the castle that looms above the entire city. Its black spiraling towers, shining slate roofs and shimmering silver windows make it stand out anywhere that I am in the city. It was made that way, to make sure we always know who is ruling us. The immortal Fae Queen. Our queen lives in that palace and has done her entire immortal life. Thousands of years, if the history books are right and our longest reigning queen to date. She keeps us safe from the dangers outside the walls of the city, from the Wyern King and his clan of Wyerns who live over in the Forgotten Lands. They are the true monsters of our world.

A cold, salty breeze blows around me, and I shiver as I pull myself from my thoughts and look back up at the building where I go every single day. The Enforcer Headquarters, one of twelve in the city, and they all look the exact same. Symmetrical pillars line the outline of the two-story building that stretches far back. Perfectly trimmed bushes make a square around the bottom floor, and three staircases lead up to the platform outside the enormous main door. All of it is black, from the stone to the bushes, except for the white door, which is always open and always guarded by new junior enforcers. I walk up the hundred and fifty-two steps to the doors, and both the enforcers nod at me, letting me in without needing to check my I.D. I'm sure they have heard of me—and not in a good way. My list of fuckups is a mile long.

I glance at the young enforcer, a woman with cherry red lipstick and black hair, and wonder why she chose to sign up to be an enforcer. I doubt she was like me, fresh out of the foster system and left with no other decent options but this. Many don't want this job, and with the right schooling, they don't have to take it. It's hard work and long hours... and we die a lot. I've been lucky to skirt death myself a few times, and each time, I thank the dragon goddess for saving me. I smile at the junior enforcer and walk into the building, across the shiny black marble floors and up to the receptionist, Wendy, who sits behind a wall of glass and a small, tidy oak desk. I like Wendy, who is part witch, but I don't hold that against her. Her black hair is curled up and pinned into a bun, and she is wearing a long blue skirt and a white chemise top. "Hello, Calliophe. I missed you yesterday during the quarter term meeting."

"Sorry about that. Monster hunting and all," I say with a genuine smile even if I'm not sorry at all for missing another boring meeting. "Is he in there?"

She nods at the steps by the side of her office that lead up to the only full floor office on the top level. All the rest of us have our offices below his. The boss made sure that he had the only room above when he was transferred here a year ago. Her dark, nearly black eyes flicker nervously. "Upstairs. He's not in a great mood tonight."

"Brilliant," I tightly say and take a deep breath. "Thanks, Wendy. See you around if I survive the boss's bad mood."

"Good luck," she whispers to me before I walk to the stairs and head up to the top level. I'm glad I took the time to quickly get changed into a black tank top and high-waisted black jeans. My pink hair flows around my shoulders to the middle of my back, reminding me that I need a haircut soon.

When I get to the top of the stairs, I pause to

look over the gigantic space that I'm rarely invited into, noticing how it smells like him. Masculine, minty and cool, which suits the space he has claimed. Massive floor-to-ceiling windows stretch across the back area, giving magnificent views of the fae castle upon the hill and the rest of the city below it. The towers, the small buildings, the people are easy to see from this vantage point. The sun slowly sets off in the distance, casting cascades of mandarin, lemony yellow and scarlet red light across the tips of buildings and across the shiny black floor. The light spreads across my boots as I walk into the room and finally look over at him. He is sitting at his desk, the single piece of furniture in this whole massive space, and on the desk is a Flame.

Flames are small red gnomes that use flames to travel from one place to another, and in general, are useful pests. The city is full of them, and for a coin, they will send a message for you. I've heard that you can ask the Flames to send anything you want, even death, to another, but it comes with a price only the dragon goddess herself could bear. They are ancient creatures and not to be messed with. I wouldn't dare ask for more than a message, and not many would.

The Flame looks back at me with its soulless black eyes, and then he disappears in a flicker of flames, leaving embers bouncing across the desk.

Merrick looks up at me with his gorgeous dark grey eyes, and the room becomes tense. Some would say his eyes are colorless, but I don't think that's true. His eyes are a perfect reflection of any color in the room, and there are others that claim his grey eyes suggest he has angelic blood. Which is laughable. The Angelic Children, a race so rare we hardly ever see them, are said to be endlessly kind.

There's nothing nice or kind about Merrick Night. My boss. His dark brown hair is perfectly gelled into place, not a stray daring to be wrong, and it's much like the expensive black suit, the perfect black tie, flawless white shirt tucked into black trousers he wears, all of it expensive. He doesn't wear the enforcer leathers, magically made material, and he has never explained why.

I stop before his desk and cross my arms.

"Do you want to explain yourself, or should I start, Miss Sprite?"

His deep, cocky, arrogant voice irritates me as we both know he knows what happened—

and why. But fine, if we are going to play this game.

I resist the urge to glower at my boss, not wanting to get fired, as I lift my chin. "I'll start, boss. We were told it was a simple monster on the loose on the left side of the city—Yenrtic District. It was suggested that an exiled werewolf had murdered mortals, and they called us to take him in. That was all that we were told, and we went to hunt him as per our job. He might have been part werewolf once, but he wasn't anymore when we found him. He was a hybrid, twisted and changed into something indescribable, but I'm sure we can go take a visit if you wish to see it."

"That won't be necessary, Miss Sprite," he coldly replies, running his eyes over me once.

I grit my teeth. "It was a difficult mission. We were underprepared for it, and none of the usual tactics for taking down a shifter worked. It went a little wrong from the start, and I do apologize for that."

"A little wrong," he slowly repeats my answer.

Here we go.

He stands up from his desk and walks over to his window. "Come with me."

I reluctantly follow him over, standing at his side as he towers over me. I hate being short at times. "A little wrong is when you make a small mistake that no one notices what you did and it doesn't attract attention. M.A.D. is known for discreetly dealing with supernaturals who have turned into monsters, for the queen. Destroying two buildings would suggest it went very wrong and quite the opposite of what your job stands for."

"Boss—"

"And furthermore, my boss is breathing down my neck to fire you. He is questioning why two of my junior associates have somehow managed to destroy two fucking expensive buildings. Explain it to me. Now, Miss Sprite."

"Technically, the monster destroyed the buildings when it had a tantrum and reacted badly to the enchanted wolfbane," I quietly answer.

"If you were struggling, you should have sent for help," he commands. "Not taken it on yourself with a new enforcer."

"We didn't have time, or it would have

escaped and killed more mortals," I sharply reply. "Isn't that the real job? To save lives?"

An awkward silence drifts between us, and I steel my back for his reply. "You're meant to be instructing your partner on how to responsibly take on monsters. What you did today was teach her that you can take on a hybrid, alone, and somehow survive by the skin of your teeth. When she goes out and repeats your lesson alone, she will be hurt. Even die."

Guilt presses down on my chest. "But, boss—"

"Yes, Miss Sprite?" he interrupts, challenging me to say anything but *I'm sorry* with those cold grey eyes of his. When I first met Merrick Night, I thought he was the most beguiling mortal I'd ever met. Then he opened his perfectly shaped lips and made me want to punch him.

I look away first and over the city, the last bits of light dying away over the horizon. "There's been so many of these hybrid creatures recently, all over Wyvcelm. I have contacts in Junepit and Goldway City who told me as much. Where are they coming from? What caused them to be like that?"

"That is classified, Miss Sprite," he coolly

replies. Basically, it's well above my pay grade to ask.

"It's probably not safe for everyone to go out in twos on missions like this anymore," I counter.

"Your only defense is that you secured the monster without Miss Mist using her voice," he says with a hint of cool amusement. "That would have been a real fuckup for us all to deal with."

Fuckup would be an understatement. The sirens' most deadly power, among many, is their enchanted voice when they sing the old language of the fae. Instantly, she would lure every male in the entire vicinity towards her, monster or not, and they would bow to her alone. Mortal females like me would be left screaming for the dragon goddess to save us, holding our hands over our ears, begging for death. Her voice stretches for at least two to three miles, and only a full-blooded fae can resist it. I've only heard it once, and personally, I never want to hear it again. I can still hear it now, like an old echo that draws me to her, a flash of the old power of the sirens who used to rule this world before the fae rose to power.

"Am I fired or can I leave, boss?"

He links his fingers, leaning back in the chair, which creaks. "I'm itching to dock your pay for this. But I won't. Not this time. You can go."

"Thank you," I say sarcastically and turn on my heel.

"Miss Sprite?" I stop mid-step and look back at him. "Don't make me regret being lenient on you today. You should know better."

I nod before turning away. "Fucking asshole," I whisper under my breath. He's not supernatural, and I know he can't hear me, and it's not like I can actually call him that to his face. Then I'd be fired for sure. Still, I'm sure I hear him chuckle under his breath.

I rush down the steps and say goodbye to Wendy before leaving the enforcement building and going to the Royal Bank on the other side of the market. I withdraw my day's pay, wincing that it's not nearly as much as I need, but a few hundred coins will sort everything out, and I'll work a double shift at the end of this week so I can eat for the rest of the week.

After making my way through the market and grabbing some dried meats, I head into the complex where my apartment is, listening to the old tower creak and groan in the wind. My apartment is four hundred and seven out of eight hundred flats in the entire building, and it is owned by the Fae Queen, like everything else. I'm lucky I got a place here, in a decent side of town, and it is everything I've worked towards for a very long time. I take the steps two at a time until I get to the hundred level. The corridor is littered with bikes, toys and plants, like every family level.

I knock twice on door one hundred and seven before opening it up with my key and heading inside.

"It's just me," I shout out as I feel how cold it is in here and flick on the magical heating. The weather is always changing so quickly. Some say it's the old gods anger that changes the weather from hot to cold all within a day. I'll pay that bill later, either way. "Louie?"

"Here," Louie shouts back, and I follow his shout to find him in the open-plan kitchen-living area, also where he has a small bed pushed up at the one side. The walls are cracked, the cream paper peeling off, but it's the same in most of the apartments. Louie is sitting on the bed, throwing an orange ball in the air and catching it over and over. Louie catches the ball one more time before sitting up, brushing locks of his black hair out of his eyes.

"How was school?" I question, leaning against the wall.

"Boring and predictable. Mr. French told me I was too smart for the class and suggested I join the fae army. Again," he tells me, and my heart lurches for a second until I see him chuckle. "I'm not crazy. Obviously."

After the age of ten, any male or female can join the fae army and be trained to fight for the queen, but they have to take the serum. The serum is an enchanted concoction that turns any mortal into a full-blooded fae and forces a bond between whoever takes it and the queen. Meaning that no one who takes the serum can ever betray her. I once thought about joining the fae army myself when things were rough and I was starving, but I will never forget the other foster kids in the homes who died from the serum. Roughly ten percent survive. I will never let Louie take a risk like that. Not even for the riches and security and the promise of power that the Fae Queen offers up.

I'm lost in my thoughts. I don't even notice

Louie climb off his bed and come over to me. His eyes are like molten silver, just like his father's were. "You look tired."

"Hello, good to see you, too. How's your mom today?"

"The same," he quietly says, walking past me and opening the door to her bedroom. His mom was once a foster mom of mine, and the only one alive. I look down at her in her bed, her thin body covered in an unnatural blue glow as she lightly hovers off the bedsheets. Five years ago, we were attacked by the monster who has hunted me my entire life. Five years ago, her mate jumped in front of her to save her life, they smashed through a wall, and she hit her head on the edge of a door. My foster dad was the only reason I became an enforcer—because he was one. The Enforcer Guild paid for this apartment and a magically protected sleep until she can be woken, not that we can afford to do that, and the Guild's sympathy only stretched so far.

This was my eleventh foster home, the very last one I went to before I turned sixteen and aged out. I remember coming here, fearful, and meeting Louie, who hugged me. I hadn't been hugged in years, and it shocked me. It was still one of the happiest days of my life.

I go over to her side, stroking her greying red hair and sighing. I'd do anything to be able to afford to wake her up. For Louie. For me.

I leave three quarters of my wages on the side, and Louie looks down at the money, right as his stomach grumbles. I smile and nod. "Should I go and get something for us?" he asks.

"And for the week. For you," I tell him, ruffling his hair.

"Thank you," he says quietly. "One day, I'm going to be an enforcer like you and pay you back for all these years. I'm going to protect you."

"You're my brother in every way that matters, and family don't owe each other debts like this," I gently tell him. "And with how smart you are, I hope to the goddess you become someone so much better than me."

"Impossible," he says with a grin.

"Be careful on the streets," I warn him as he picks up a few of the coins and shoves them into his faded brown trousers. I need to buy him some new clothes soon, judging from the tears and holes in his blue shirt. One thing I love about Louie is that he never complains, never asks for clothes or for anything that costs money except for food. I wish I could give him more, but I can't.

"The monsters can't catch me, I'm too fast," he exclaims before bolting out of the door.

I chuckle as I sit down in the chair by the side of her bed, picking up her pale hand. "He doesn't have a clue, does he, mom? But he looks so much like dad."

Silence and the gentle hum of the magic surrounding her is my only reply, and I can't even remember what her voice is like anymore. She was my foster mom for a few years, far longer than any of the other ten before her, and she always asked me to call her *mom*. "One day, I'm going to wake you up so you can see Louie growing into a strong man. I'm going to make sure he gets a good job and stays far away from the true dangers of this city."

I hope she can hear me. I hope it gives her some comfort to know I'm here, but a part of me wonders if she would resent me. I'm the reason she is like this. I'm the reason her mate is dead. I close my eyes and blow out a shaky breath. The monster hasn't come back, not for years, and I have no reason to suspect he will now. But if he does, this time, I won't be a helpless child, unable to stop him from murdering my foster parents. I don't know if he killed my biological parents, no one does, but he killed every enforcer family that took me in. I try not to think of it, of all the death that haunted me like he did. My monster, my lurking shadow. I stay with my foster mom for a little longer before cleaning up the house, doing the washing and tidying in her room before Louie gets back, and then we cook dinner together before eating.

"Can I come to yours to play a game of kings?" he asks, referring to the card game we play on quiet nights, especially weekends like today, as I wash up and he dries the plates.

"I'd usually have you over, but I'm meeting Nerelyth for drinks tonight. It's her birthday," I tell him softly. Most kids his age would prefer to play with their friends and have them over, but Louie has never been good at making friends. He keeps to himself.

"Okay," he replies, his voice tinged with sadness. Loneliness. He only has me and his mom, but she can't read him stories, play games and help with the complicated enchantment work he is learning at school. After grabbing my bag, I kiss the top of his head before I leave, closing the door behind me and resting my head back against it, my eyes drooping. I'm so tired and I could use a long nap, not a night of partying for Nerelyth's birthday.

I sigh and push myself off the wall before heading up to my apartment. It is partially paid for by the Enforcer Guild, one of the half decent things they do for their employees. The night sky glitters like a thousand moons as I get to my floor and look up at the sunroof far above. Three actual moons hang in the sky somewhere, but I can't see them from here, and I wish I could. They say looking at the three moons and making a wish is the only way for the dragon goddess to hear you. I'm sure it's not true, but I still look up sometimes and wish. I shove my key into the lock, wondering if I have any enchanted wine left over from last time Nerelyth came over, and push into my cold apartment. If I get dressed quickly, I might even have time to finish the extremely spicy romance book I was reading last night, on the way to the bar.

"Posy, where are you?" I shout out as I head in. "I bought some of those meat strips you like from the market, as I'm going out tonight with Nerelyth. It's her birthday, remember?"

I've been mostly absent for the last two days and not had much time to spend with Posy—my roommate who happens to be a bat and stuck that way thanks to a witch's curse. I drop my bag on the side and look around in the darkness before sighing. Clicking my fingers, balls of warm white light within small glass spheres flood my apartment with light from where they are attached to the wall. I search around the main area, a small kitchen with two counters, a magical food storage box, and a large worn sofa pressed against the wall. It looks nearly the same as when I moved in, I notice, except for my two bookcases in the corridor leading to the bathroom and bedroom, full of romance books I've collected over the years. My prized possessions.

Escapism at its finest.

"Posy, come on. You can't still be mad at me?" I holler in frustration as I walk into the tiny bathroom, which is empty. "Bats are nocturnal, so I know you're awake and ignoring me, but I don't have time to chase you around this apartment all night."

I hear a small rustling noise from my

bedroom, and I smile as I walk over and push the door open.

Clicking my fingers, two lights burn to life above my bed, and I go still. My heart nearly stops because it's not Posy in my bedroom.

There's a monster sitting on my bed.

## CHAPTER 30
# BONUS READ

Large wings.

Grey skin.

Muscular, massive shoulders and thick arms.

"Get the hell out!" I shout, a scream dying in my throat as I take a step away. I pull my dagger out from the clip on my thigh and hold it out between us as I quickly look for Posy, not seeing her anywhere. There's a friggin' monster in my room.

A wave of magic whips into my hand, the sting of it cold and piercing. My dagger flips across the room as I flinch, and it embeds itself in the wall with a thud. The monster doesn't even lift its head. He's... reading—my spicy romance book, of all things—as he sits on my bed. My double bed looks tiny with him sitting there, his dark hair soft and curling down his shoulders.

What the fuck?

My eyes widen as I look at this monster. He's a male. That much I'm sure of, and he's huge. He's sitting in the middle of my bed, reading my book from last night, looking like he's meant to be there. His skin is dark grey and almost velvety. Massive black wings stretch out of his back, but they're pulled in at his sides. Black horns curl out of the top of his thick black hair on his head, and if he wasn't a monster, I might even say he's handsome. He's shirtless, and he has pants on, but a tiny weird part of me focuses on the lack of a shirt for a second. No one looks that good shirtless—except this monster, it seems.

He is so big, and I'm sure he could snap me like a twig. Who the hell is he? What is he? More importantly—why is he in my bedroom?

"This is an interesting book for an innocent doe like you to be reading, Calliophe Maryann Sprite."

I freeze, my heart pounding as his deep,

sensual voice fills my room. How does he know my full name?

He looks up at me with hauntingly beautiful amethyst eyes and smirks. "Speechless, Doe?"

"Get the fuck out of my room!" I shout, grabbing the nearest thing on my side table and throwing it at him. He catches the stuffed purple teddy bear in his hand, then raises an eyebrow as his lips twitch with humor.

"Don't run," he purrs.

I glare as I grab the next thing, which is a cheap statue of the goddess, and I throw that straight at him instead. The statue crashes into his hand, smashes into pieces on impact, and he simply sighs in annoyance as he begins to stand. My old bed creaks as I grab my precious books from the corridor as I back away and throw them at him as I retreat. He catches them all like it's a game. I can't hear anything but my heartbeat, and I can't see anything but those wings that have haunted me for so many years. My monster had wings. It's all I can remember of him before he killed every parent I ever had.

Wings. The beat of wings fills my ears as I burn with anger. My monster is back to kill me. I turn and run to the sofa, jumping on it as I pull out the two daggers I have hidden down on one side and crouch down in the corner. He casually strolls down the corridor, and he blocks the way to the only exit from my apartment as he faces me and crosses his arms. "Do you really believe that you, a tiny little mortal, will be able to stop me?"

"Come closer. Find out," I taunt. If he is going to kill me, I'm going down with a fight. I haven't survived monsters all these years, my entire life, to die easily at the hands of one.

He laughs, the sound deep and frightening. Arrogant son of a bitc—

I see a flash of black right before Posy flies straight into his face, clawing at him with her tiny, almost purple, bat wings. Posy is only a tiny bat and no more than the size of his hand as he grabs her by the scruff of her neck and holds her up in front of him. She still fights. The more I look at him, I realize he can't be the monster who hunted me. Those purple eyes aren't black, dark and cold like my monster's were. Still, those wings... my monster must be what he is. "What is this thing?" he asks.

I would laugh if he wasn't trying to kill me. Posy yells, "Die, die, die. You supernatural monster! This is my home, and I don't care how horny my roommate is. She is not fucking a monster when I'm living here!"

By the old gods. My cheeks burn.

The monster smirks and looks over at me. "You have a talking bat."

"Let her go!" I demand as I look between them and the door. I don't know how I will make it to the door to run if I go for Posy.

He sighs, and Posy is still ranting away, unaware that no one is listening to her anymore. Or the fact this monster isn't my date and that he is here to kill me. "No. We are leaving."

"We are not," I say at the same time Posy declares, "Finally. Go to the monster's place and do the dirty. Between keeping me here as your pet and your new fuck buddy, I think you have a weird thing for bats."

"We bats can be very fun," the monster agrees with a hint of dry amusement that makes him seem almost mortal. Almost. He is very much not.

He lets Posy go, and she flies into my bedroom, slamming the door shut. I need a better roommate/pet. Posy sucks.

"Then go and have fun somewhere else, or

I'm going to pin those nice wings of yours to my wall," I say, holding the daggers up higher. Why he hasn't used his magic to rid me of them yet floats into the back of my mind. Maybe he is playing with me. "What are you, anyway?"

"Wyern," he coolly answers. "Haven't you seen any in your career?"

No, I haven't, or I'd be very dead. My blood runs cold as I take him in, a Wyern male, in my living room. The Wyerns are immortal, deadly, and everyone knows they are forbidden from entering Ethereal City. Some say they are fae—an old race of them. Some say they were created by the fae and are born monsters.

I should have known he's not a monster. Not exactly, but not far from one. From what I know, the Wyerns live in the Forgotten Lands, a punishment from my queen for the war they started thousands of years ago. Some say the sirens siding with the Fae Queen was the only way we won.

One trained Wyern male can slaughter ten trained fae in minutes.

My heart races as I take all of this in. If I call for help and they find me here with him, even if he is trying to kill me or take me somewhere, the queen will execute me for treason. "If the queen finds you here, which she will, we are both dead. Leave."

He steps towards me, an amused smirk on his lips. "Your precious queen would be very honored if I turned up in her city, but perhaps a little angry I came for you and not to see her."

"What?"

He glowers at me. "Are you mortals truly this dense? We. Are. Leaving."

"We certainly are not going anywhere!"

He takes another step forward, and I start to back away until the back of my knees touch the sofa.

I lash out at him with my daggers, cutting through his arm, and it bubbles with blood. He doesn't even notice as he grabs my hands, squeezing tight enough I'm forced to drop the daggers with a yelp. I kick at his shin, which is like a rock and only hurts me, and he grabs me by the waist and throws me over his shoulder like I weigh nothing. I scream and kick him in the stomach and slam my hands on his solid back, but nothing makes his arm shift from his iron tight grip on me.

Magic wraps around me firmly, its icy sting

burning into my skin, and I hiss in pain as my head spins. I hate magic.

"Let me go!" I scream over and over. He only laughs like it's deeply amusing to him as he walks out of my apartment by kicking my front door open. I look up in horror as he spreads his massive wings out, and magic lashes around us as he shoots up the flights of stairs. The stairs whip up around us as I scream, ducking my head as my stomach feels like a million butterflies have burst to life. He crashes through the glass, bits of it cutting into my arms, and launches us into the night sky above the city. His wings beat near my face, and I stop trying to fight him. If he drops me, I'm dead.

It doesn't stop the lash of magic that slams into my head and knocks me out cold seconds later, leaving me dreaming of wings and star-filled night skies.

# CHAPTER 31
# BONUS READ

"*Take her, Vivienne. Just take her and run!*"

*I snuggle down into my bed, clutching the sheets tighter as I hear crashing noises, shouting and doors slamming. It's happening again. He has come for me again. No, no, no...*

"*We both can run and fight him,*" *my foster mom pleads. I've only been here a year. It's too soon for the monster to come for me.*

"*No. She needs someone to live for her,*" *my foster dad exclaims, and the door to my room slams. "She is just six years old, and all she has known is death. Someone has to tell her why, someone has to explain the truth.*"

*"He'll never stop," Vivienne cries. "We shouldn't have taken her in after—"*

*"I have no regrets. We do this for the Guild. For our queen and what she gave," he interrupts her. Hands pull my quilt back, and I look up at my foster dad with panicked eyes. His voice is gentle and as soft as his brown eyes as he stares down at me. "You need to go with Vivienne and run. It's here, and I'm going to stop it."*

*"But—"*

*He hushes me, kissing my forehead. "It's been an honor to care for you, Calliophe Maryann Sprite. Live."*

*I gulp, tears falling down my cheeks as Vivienne picks me up, holding me to her. She always picks me up, telling me how small I am for my age, and I cling to her neck, wishing this is all a dream. It's not real. The monster isn't real.*

*I hide my head in her bright red hair, peeping out to look at my foster dad standing by the door. He looks over his shoulder, holding a silver sword in front of him, an enchanted rope dangling from his fingers. "Live for all of us, Calliophe."*

*Vivienne and he share a look for a moment before she carries me to the window, and my foster dad opens the door, shutting it behind us. Vivienne opens the window before sitting on the edge, the icy wind blowing around us, snowflakes littering the air. My breath comes out like smoke as I shiver. "Hold on to me and don't let go."*

*I nod against her shoulder as she jumps off the window ledge into the snowy night, and I cling to her as she lands in a thump on the ground. Vivienne wraps her arms around me before she sprints across the grass, leaping over the small brown fence and past the swing tied to the old oak tree. I keep looking over her shoulder for the monster inside my home, but no lights are on, and there is nothing but the glittering night sky until I hear a male scream.*

*Vivienne stops and slowly turns back, holding me tightly to her. She puts me down on the ground and points at the woods a few feet away. "I have to go back for him. I love him. You have to run. Don't stop running. Find someone, anyone, and tell them to call the Guild. Tell them we're in trouble, but you need to run."*

*"I don't want to be on my own," I wail as she lowers me to the ground, pulling my arms from her and stepping back.*

*She kisses my forehead. "I'm so sorry, but he is all I have."*

*"You have me."*

*I try to catch her hand, but she pushes me away before she runs back to the house. Tears fall down my cheeks, and I shake from head to toe as I turn and run into the tall, dark trees. I cling to the nearest tree, the bark scratching my hands and the branches snatching in my hair. Everything is silent for a moment before I hear Vivienne scream and cry out, and then there is silence once more. I hear a door being smashed open, and I turn to see a male stepping out into the shadows. He has gigantic wings that spread out like shadows in the night, but I can't see anything else as he turns my way.*

*Terrified, I run deep into the forest, letting it swallow me in its darkness.*

I wake up with my heart racing fast in my chest as I blink and look around, tasting the icy sting of magic on my tongue. It was just a dream. I click my fingers, and lights burn up in the room, and I go still.

It wasn't a dream.

I've been kidnapped by that arrogant, and a little beautiful, monster. The bat guy. Shit. I take in the scents around me on the soft sheets, and I frown. Masculine. This is that monster's bedroom. By the goddess. I push the dark midnight blue sheets off me, noticing my boots are missing as I look at the bedroom. Expensive and exotic wood makes the massive bed I'm on, and there are matching wardrobes and a dresser. They go well with the dark red walls and polished oak beams that run across the ceiling and the carmine curtains. I look back at the headboard, which is one magnificent piece of wood carved and polished.

My legs are shaky from the magic and a little fear as I walk across the hardwood floors and to the window. The window is massive, ceiling to floor, with black squares all over it. My heart stops as I look outside at the unfamiliar mountains.

We aren't in Ethereal City.

If I had to guess where I am... The Wyern are said to live in the Forgotten City, in the thick mountains to the north of Ethereal City. I've only ever seen these mountains from a far distance, and then they were nothing more than a dot on the horizon. Now, I'm in the middle of them. The mountains are steep, covered in jagged spikes and snow. It's kind of pretty, with the night sky hanging behind, the sun slowly rising.

I think it's safe to bet I'm not going to work today.

My heart is still racing, and I will myself to calm down. If the Wyern wanted me dead, I would be dead. No, he must want me for something else, and that gives me time to make a plan and escape.

Somehow.

I glance around to see if I can find anything useful to defend myself, but there isn't much, just a dresser, two wardrobes, and a rug. I search the wardrobe and drawers, finding male clothes and nothing else. Unless I plan to throw socks at him, my search isn't going well. I find my boots by the end of the bed and slide them on, finding the two small knives I hid in the heel have been taken. My mouth feels dry as I go to the dark wooden double doors and test the silver handles to see if I'm locked in. The doors click open to my surprise, and I peek out into the corridor. The same dark wood floor stretches down a long and wide passageway, and there's a dark red, patterned runner running down the entire length of it. There are endless doors on either side and more light orbs lighting up the space on the ceiling. I hear vague scuffling, voices and music from the left side, and the right is completely empty and silent but a dead end by the looks of it.

I quietly shut the door behind me as I step out and head down the passageway, wishing I had some of my weapons on me. I try a few handles on my way, but all of them are locked, to my annoyance.

I blow out a shaky breath when I see a door open a few feet away, the noise coming from in there and orange light shining out the gap. My hair falls around my shoulders, and I tuck a strand behind my ear as I follow the sounds of the music. It's old music, but it's sensual and soft and not what I expect to hear. I walk the final steps to the door and peek into the massive room. Pillars and tapestries line the walls, all of it old and stunning, and the soft music is being played by magic throughout the air, the taste of it coating my tongue. Several cushioned areas lie around three giant waterfalls with statues of the goddess in the center of them, water pouring out of her hands. The room is warm and cozy, but maybe not the people inside it. Wyerns. Each one of them looks slightly different, all dark or grey skinned, and there are at least twenty female mortals in here with them. By the moans, they're clearly having fun, and I try not to look too long at any one of them. They are all having sex.

Except a few. Like the male on the seating area nearest me. He is different from the others; his light grey skin is littered with small and large scars, and his horns have been cut off. He doesn't have wings, and his eyes are a soft forest green as he looks my way. He has a grey shirt on that a female with long brown hair is pawing at. In fact, he has three females lying on his lap, and one of them is stroking him underneath his trousers. He still watches me, tilting his head to the side with a little smirk on his lips as one of the other females runs her hand through his short brown hair. Dear god, I just walked into a monster orgy. Absolutely brilliant. I really hope that is not what they brought me here for. I haven't had sex with anyone for over two years thanks to my work. And even then, I prefer a heated few hours at their place and then I disappear. I don't do long-term anything.

I'm certainly not staying here if this is the plan.

"The doe is awake," the male shouts, and many male laughs follow. Fuck it.

I push the door open and head inside, letting the door slam against the wall. "Kidnapping is illegal. I'm leaving if one of you will be kind enough to show me the door."

"I don't think so, little doe," the male says, gently pushing the females off him and standing. He walks up to me, towering over me. "We've been waiting for you to wake up. Do you want a drink?"

I glower at him. "No."

"Come on, relax. Have you never seen a royal court having fun before?"

"This is a royal court?" I say dryly. "Looks more like—"

"Ah, be nice. You don't insult someone's home when you're a guest," he interrupts.

"I'm not a guest. I didn't come here willingly!" I protest.

"Still, be nice, little mortal."

He pats me on the head and looks back at the beautiful females on the sofa, who giggle. By the goddess. It stinks of sex in here, and the moans are getting louder than the music. "No."

"How about that drink?"

"No," I repeat, and he smiles at me. "I want

to know why I'm here? Where's the male that kidnapped me and took me?"

He sighs, stepping closer, and offers me his hand. He smells of wine and bad decisions. Nerelyth would love him. "My name is Lorenzo Eveningstar."

I don't take it, considering what he has just been doing, and raise an eyebrow. He chuckles deep and low. "Usually when someone tells you their name, you shake their hand and tell them your name. Do mortals like yourself no longer know manners?"

"So you don't know my name? After kidnapping me—"

"I didn't kidnap you," he quickly corrects me.

I rub my forehead. "My name is Calliophe."

"Ah, I did wonder if it was Doe," he smiles and looks me over. "I don't know what my king is thinking."

King?

The Wyern King kidnapped me?

By the goddess, I'm dead. I'm so dead.

I cross my arms with bravado I don't have. "Why am I here, Lorenzo?"

"I believe that is for King Emerson Eveningstar to answer," another voice answers.

I turn to look over at the female walking towards me. She's fae. This female is a full-blooded fae. She's wearing pretty much nothing but a slip of silver sheer fabric that makes up a dress that is wrapped around her large breasts and thin waist before falling to her feet. She is flawless. Fae always are. Everything about them is designed to trick mortals like myself into trusting them. Her beautiful silvery blonde hair that is loosely held up, curls and falls around her shoulders and slender face. She stops in front of me, and her eyes light up in different shades of purple and blue.

Lorenzo smiles at the fae female. "Calliophe, meet another member of our court, Zurine Quarzlin. Rine, she is looking for Emerson."

Zurine looks me over from the top of my head to my feet, focusing on my eyes for a second. I search her eyes and see nothing but sadness hidden within them. "Why don't I show you the way?"

My smile is tight. "Alright."

She waves her hand at the door, and I follow her through, glancing back to see Lorenzo swaggering back to the females. "I imagine you're confused and worried, but ignore the males here.

As usual, they think with their cocks and not their minds half the time, much like the rest of our court. That's not why he brought you here. The mortal females come to our court willingly for the pleasure."

I dryly chuckle. "Confused? I was kidnapped by a monster."

"My king isn't a monster," she says softly, her voice full of affection. "Even if he appears as one."

"I hadn't seen a Wyern before, so to me, he looked like one. Then he kidnapped me...," I drawl.

She laughs lightly as we head down the corridor, and our conversation drifts off until I need to fill the silence instead of feeling so nervous. "I haven't seen many fae before. Only one or two. Most don't come down to the lower parts of Ethereal City, and my work doesn't lead me anywhere near the castle or the fae district."

She doesn't look down at me. "Then you are lucky, mortal."

"Perhaps," I mutter. "So you're part of this court even when you're not one of them?"

She looks at me this time as we go through a door and into a corridor with long windows on each side. "Yes, and for what it is worth, you can trust me. You won't be able to trust many here."

One of these Wyerns is my monster, hunted me from birth, and I won't trust anyone here until I find who it is. And kill them.

"For what it's worth, I don't believe trusting anyone here is going to end with anything but my death."

She smiles at that. "You're a smart mortal."

Weird compliment.

"Although you're not all mortal, are you? You definitely have a bit of fae in your bloodline with those eyes. Who was it?"

I look at the shiny floor. "I don't know any of my family."

"Oh, I'm sorry. Is your hair natural or enchanted?"

"Enchanted by a dodgy spell, and I haven't been able to change it back since I was fifteen," I explain with a chuckle. "It was a lesson in why you don't buy enchantments from strangers on the market."

She laughs. "I think pink is your color."

I smile for a moment at the fae female. "Thank you."

She leads me down several corridors,

through a few more empty rooms, each more confusing than the last until I'm thoroughly lost. We both stay silent until we come to a massive pair of imposing doors at the end of a corridor. These are curved to almost look like bat wings, and they are old, much like the walls around it. Zurine pulls the doors open and moves to the side. "I'll leave you to him. Remember, with these males, they will bite if you push too much."

She lowers her voice. "But most of them have a soft heart underneath it all. Especially the king."

I walk into the gigantic room, eyeing the red carpet that runs up to a platform at the back of the room, where a king sits on a massive throne. The throne is made of black oak, with five long spikes making the headboard that looks like the spiked mountains outside. The throne room, which I'm guessing this is, is magnificent. Pillars line the walls with windows between them, lined with black squares. Fae light, a rare and expensive form of magic, hovers in tiny little stars across the entire ceiling, and it makes it look like the endless night sky.

Beautiful and daunting.

I turn my gaze to the throne, pulled towards it with an invisible tug deep in my chest.

The king sits on his throne, his legs spread wide, his wings hanging off the sides of the seat. Tight black leathers spread across his chest and down his arms, and into his leather trousers. The shine of the leather reminds me that they must be enchanted, maybe by himself. I'm not sure what powers the Wyerns have, but if they can effortlessly fight the fae, making enchantments should be nothing. His hand is dug into the brown hair of a female between his knees, her head resting on his knee. The room smells of sex, and looking at the pair of them, it's clear what they have been doing. The female doesn't even look at me as she stares up at Emerson, and he tilts his head to the side as his eyes lock on mine. The move is pure predator-like with a stillness only an immortal can have. "What do you want?"

I shiver from his deep, cold voice, but I don't cower. "That's the very question I came to ask you. Considering you kidnapped me."

He stands up off his throne with fury in his eyes, leaving the female on her knees, and walks towards me with a casualness that makes me fear him. He is so tall I have to arch my neck to look at him as he stops close. "Mortals bow to kings. Get on your knees."

"No," I bite out.

A lash of magic slams into my knees, and I fall to my knees before the king, unwillingly, and I glare at him as his magic surrounds me, holding me in place.

He looks down at me like I'm a bug to a bird flying high above. To him, I might as well be. "Next time I tell you to bow, you bow. Next time I tell you anything, you do it. Welcome to my court, Doe. Stay here."

He walks past me, leaving me locked in his magic as the mortal female rushes past me to follow him out. Only when the throne room doors slam shut behind me does the magic fade away, and I bite back the urge to scream.

I really, really hate the king.

Made in United States
Cleveland, OH
13 February 2026